339 m

K

O

15 m

R

A

3451 m

LAKE PLATEAU

ABSAROKA
BEARTOOTH

in National Forest

3261 m

D0130822

THE SHELTER CYCLE

ALSO BY PETER ROCK

My Abandonment

The Unsettling: Stories

The Bewildered

The Ambidextrist

Carnival Wolves

This Is the Place

The Shelter Cycle

PETER ROCK

Houghton Mifflin Harcourt

BOSTON   NEW YORK

2013

For information about permission to reproduce selections from this book,
write to Permissions, Houghton Mifflin Harcourt Publishing Company,
215 Park Avenue South, New York, New York 10003.

www.hmhbooks.com

Library of Congress Cataloging-in-Publication Data
Rock, Peter, date.
The Shelter Cycle / Peter Rock.
pages cm
ISBN 978-0-547-85908-8
1. Church Universal and Triumphant — Fiction. 2. Children — Montana — Fiction.
3. Self-realization — Fiction. I. Title.
PS3568.O327S54 2013
813'.54 — dc23   2012040363

Book design by Brian Moore

Printed in the United States of America
DOC 10 9 8 7 6 5 4 3 2 1

An excerpt of this book originally appeared in *Tin House.*

for L

THE SHELTER CYCLE

When I was out by myself in the mountains, I liked to think he was somewhere in the trees. I hiked up the canyons, over the ridge and under the pines and aspens to a place where an old cabin had been. It was only a stone chimney and foundation, all broken down. I tore out long grass for a bed, then stepped through the doorway, a gap in the stones with no walls on either side.

I could hear dogs barking, far away, when I closed my eyes. I heard the stream nearby, the wind in the leaves above. And I heard my name. *Francine, Francine.*

He stood in the doorway. Wearing his dark blue Cub Scout shirt, the patches on his pocket and his jeans with holes in the knees. Colville Young. He pretended to knock on the door, then stepped inside and stretched out next to me on the bed of grass. We were ten years old, eleven. He was shorter, and his arms were too long for his body, and his hair was almost white, even lighter than mine.

High above, the aspens' leaves slapped, the blue sky bright between them. I listened to Colville's breathing, trying to match mine to it. My shoulder felt his shoulder, even though we didn't touch. I turned my head, his ear so close to my mouth. When I moved my fingers down along my side, they touched his, and we both pulled away.

Eyes closed, we listened to the stream, its liquid sounds the voices of Undines, the nature spirits who served water. I imagined all the Elementals looking down at the two of us, on our bed

1

of green grass. They were the servants of God and man in the planes of matter, which is where we were living, where they protected us. The Undines in the water, and the spirits that served the fire element, called Salamanders. Elementals of the earth were Gnomes. Those of the air, Sylphs.

The thoughts we had, out in nature, were actually the Elementals making their wishes seem like ours. We built tiny homes for them, filled with quartz crystal, in the little caves of the splintery cliffs. The Elementals were part of the reason our parents let us play alone out there. Our parents, they had so much to do, so many preparations to make. It was fortunate for everyone that we had spiritual protection.

What you are reading is the beginning of a letter. It is a letter to you, though I don't know when you'll be able to read it. It's also a letter to myself, to remind me of those things I might try to forget, like how it felt in those days when I was a girl, out in the mountains with Colville.

Colville and I followed deer paths, and we had our own paths, too. We walked side by side and then he went out in front with a stick, in case of rattlesnakes. As we came over the ridge, a dry wind slipped around us, and we started down the other side. The sky was wide and everywhere, full of things we could not see.

Sagebrush and cactus grew up the rock walls toward us. Far below, cars and trucks slid by on Highway 89, back and forth to Yellowstone Park. The dark river ran along next to the highway.

When we forked over into another canyon I caught a glimpse of Mount Emigrant, far away, where the pattern of the dark trees and the white snow made a kind of seahorse. I always looked for that. When I saw it, I knew I was close to home.

Around us, gray metal doors cut into hillsides. White ventilation pipes hooked out of the ground. Down the slope I could see people loading all the supplies we'd need into half-buried boxcars and, farther away, some adults atop a greenhouse, fighting with heavy plastic sheets that were blowing up and down. The rickety houses and trailers we passed were all painted shades of purple and blue.

Colville was talking about the Messenger's teachings on robots, and about space colonization, about the Mechanized Man, Atlantis, the Soviet Union. I couldn't keep up with his talk, and I didn't try. I watched the sky. I knew that Forcefields were drifting by, like floating minefields in the sea, that they could shift our moods and our energy so quickly. It made me feel vulnerable and also like I had to stay focused, to keep my energies in the right place, my attitude and intentions good all the time. That's what I was trying to do, what Colville was trying, what the Elementals were helping us with.

The country opened up as we came out of the canyon. It was so windy in the open; we always had dust in our mouths. We kept walking, past an old tepee my dad had set up, past round oil tanks that were waiting to be buried. People would live inside them, once the world all around us was no longer here.

1

IF HE'D STOLEN a girl, where would he hide her?

What a way to be thinking, to catch oneself thinking. Wells Davidson stumbled on a clump of brush; the smell of sage rose into the cold, dry air. The sky above was the palest blue. Small airplanes crisscrossed through it, searching.

Other members of his team – other neighbors, trying to help – walked ten feet on either side of him. A tall man with dark hair, wearing a ski parka over a dress shirt. A woman in a khaki outfit with a white hat like a cloth sombrero. All through the foothills of Boise, people swarmed in these organized groups. Searching, calling. From up here, Wells could see the ridge of Saddleback Park, the towers of the hospitals downtown. He could see his neighborhood, far below, the small house that he shared with his wife, Francine. He could even see the black shape of their dog, Kilo, circling the yard, next to the picnic table, looking up and probably wondering why so many people were in the hills again this afternoon.

The girl had disappeared two nights before. Nine years old, and she'd been sleeping in her back yard, on a trampoline with her younger sister, who didn't wake up until the next morning, an empty sleeping bag beside her. Wells had known the girl – her name and her sharp face, her wild black hair. She waved when she coasted down the sidewalk on her red bicycle. That was all. She lived just down the street, two houses from him and Francine.

The trampoline, at this distance, looked like a dark hole bored deep into the earth. Yesterday morning he'd looked out his kitchen window and seen three men in suits and gloves dusting for fingerprints, picking at the black mat with tweezers, photographing it.

"Hurry up," someone called. "Keep the line straight." It was the short, thick police officer who led their search team. His gun belt looked heavy, the crown of his felt hat lined dark with sweat despite the cold.

Wells had thought that one day of searching would be enough — after all, if the girl had been stolen away, it was probably in a car and she was now miles, states from here. Francine disagreed; almost eight months pregnant, she wanted to search. She thought that evidence from the trampoline or wherever else might suggest that the girl was closer. Francine was with another team now; she'd started earlier, while he was helping with the tents again. He'd listened as the sheriff spoke to the volunteers, saying, "We know in our hearts that she's alive," saying that it had been two nights but that it was quite possible that whoever had done this was sitting tight, waiting for things to quiet down so they could move farther away.

Wells glanced up just as his team met another group of searchers. The two lines slipped through each other, paths crossing at right angles. He slowed, surrounded for a moment by girls, blond girls in stocking caps and heavy coats, boots. Serious expressions on their faces, chapped lips set tight. They were the lost girl's classmates, perhaps, or from her church, or both. They didn't look up as they passed, just straight ahead, down at the ground, searching for their friend.

The wind whistled, sharp and cold. It was mid-October; if the weather had been like this two days ago, the sisters would never have slept outside on the trampoline. But it had been warmer, and they had wanted to try out their new down sleeping bags.

Plastic shell casings, a piece of cloth that wouldn't have anything to do with anything, shards of broken bottle so cloudy they looked like beach glass. Wells picked it all up with his gloved hand, slipped it into the clear plastic bag he'd been given. What would he do if he found the girl? What if she was dead? He was supposed to leave her be, to alert the others, not to touch her. But that didn't seem right somehow. If a person found his dead body in a place like this, tangled in the sagebrush with shards of sharp stones around his head or blood on his throat, he'd want them to reach out, at least to touch his shoulder, comfort him somehow, close his eyes.

They were circling back to where they'd started now. Over a slight ridge, along a line of half-finished houses, all exposed plywood and white Tyvek, construction sites cordoned off with yellow tape. The streets here weren't paved yet. Down below, all the vehicles and the orange tents stood at the end of the blacktop. Police cars lined that edge, along with an ambulance. Only police dogs were allowed on the search—a K9 truck was parked to one side—and the dogs other people had brought along were all tied together, leashes snarled. They pulled each other in and out of the shade, looking from a distance like one solid, furry mass. One barked, then another.

Wells tried to find Francine, but she wasn't around the tents. Across the hillsides, teams were still searching; she was either out there or already home, waiting for him.

He turned and headed down the curving streets. Perhaps the girl had walked up this slope, led by a person or persons, into the foothills to hide. Or perhaps she was alone, wandering off, confused, something wrong with her memory. She could be so many places.

Posters with her smiling face hung everywhere. PLEASE FIND ME. And blue ribbons had been tied in the trees' branches. The trees here in the heights, by the newer homes, were recently

7

planted, all their leaves gone. As he descended closer to his own neighborhood, the branches of the older, taller trees shook in the wind. A few yellow leaves, blown loose, spun down.

Vans from the local news stations were parked all along the curb, call numbers painted on their sides; telescopic arms with round satellite dishes rose from them. He stepped over the thick black cords that snaked everywhere, pausing to look at the girl's house, where all the cameramen pointed their lenses. It was one of the few two-story houses on the street. Clapboard, painted blue. All the curtains were drawn. He imagined the parents trapped inside, waiting for any word, the younger sister wondering why she'd been left behind.

"Are you a neighbor?" said a woman with a microphone.

He walked away without saying anything, without looking back, then turned at his driveway, went up the steps and through the side door. Kicking off his hiking boots, he took a beer from the refrigerator, leaned back against the counter, closed his eyes. He should have taken sunglasses — another day out in the brightness, squinting at everything, a headache coming on.

He opened his eyes slowly, a fraction at a time. The framed photograph of Francine's parents faced him. From long ago, back in Montana: her father wore a straw cowboy hat, a dark mustache hiding his mouth, a wrench in his hand that showed on the other side of Francine's mother, his arm around her back. She was smiling, her dark hair blown sideways in the wind, wearing a purple dress that the wind pulled at, too. They stood in front of a yellow bulldozer. Francine had pointed out to him that through the cockpit you could see the top of her head, just a girl's; her older sister Maya's arm was visible on the other side. Wells had never had the chance to meet Francine's parents. She sometimes said they would have liked him, but she never spoke much about them — she had been young, not even a teenager, when they died.

The phone rang; it took a moment for him to find it beneath the newspaper on the table.

"Is Francine there?" a man said.

"Not right now."

"I'm calling from the hospital — I'm the scheduler. We haven't heard from her."

"She's just been so involved with the search," Wells said.

"Pardon me?"

"For the missing girl," he said. "She's our neighbor. I'll have Francine call."

Out the window, Kilo still sniffed around the edges of the yard, along the fence line. Two fences over, the round black trampoline sat, surrounded by yellow tape, the scene of a crime. Wells washed his hands, splashed cold water on his face.

◆

He was sitting at the kitchen table, halfway through his second beer, when Francine returned. She wore a blue hat with a floppy brim, a tan parka, and Kilo came in the door behind her, his black tail slapping the cabinets. He licked Wells's hand, collapsed under the table, then got up and rushed off again to check something in the living room.

"You all right?" Wells said.

"I believe so." Francine's dark blond hair fell loose as she took off the hat; the light caught the pale freckles across her nose. "It feels good to be doing something, I guess."

"Someone from the hospital called," he said. "They wanted to know if you're coming back to work tomorrow."

Francine faced away from him, standing at the sink. She turned the faucet on and off, on again, letting it run for a moment. From the back she hardly looked pregnant at all — she said this was due to her height, the length of her torso. He'd always liked her broad shoulders, how strong she looked just standing in the kitchen or on the sidewalk with her neck and spine straight, those shoulders, her excellent posture.

"You've been out there all day," he said. "You shouldn't be on your feet like that."

"It's just," she said. "It's just that I keep thinking of myself when I was her age, how I felt, what I'd have done. And then I start thinking about our baby, how they can just disappear like this, no matter what you do."

"Francine."

"Look at her," she said.

"Who?"

"I heard she was out searching today."

He realized that Francine was looking through the window; over her shoulder, he could see the upstairs window of the girl's house. In that room, two houses away, the girl's little sister was jumping on a bed, up and down, her black hair loose and her hands reaching toward the ceiling.

"Do you know her name?" he said.

"Which one?"

"The little sister."

"Della?" she said. "I think that's right."

They stayed like that, watching the girl jump; they didn't say a thing until she tired herself out and climbed down. She walked away, disappearing from their view.

2

ON THE RADIO, an expert was explaining the statistics of child abduction. How many of the lost children were found, how many were taken by someone they knew, how few were still alive after four days. Wells stacked the dinner dishes and carried them to the sink. Out the window he could see the vans being packed up—men coiling cables and putting cameras into cases, headlights switching on, engines starting up.

"I guess they won't be out there much longer," he said. "Now that it's over."

"It's not over," Francine said. She sat drinking tea, her papers from work spread out in front of her. Kilo lay under the table, at her feet.

"I meant the search being called off," Wells said. "That's all. That the news people won't be out on the street."

"Unless it really is over," she said. "If it's over for the girl, like the radio says it probably is, after four days."

Wells turned on the water in the sink, turned it off before it got hot. "I was thinking," he said, "it might be nice to get away from this for a little while. Just a weekend up in the Sawtooths or something."

"I don't know."

"I mean, if you feel up to it."

"It's the time," she said. "Work. If I take time now, I won't have it later—"

There was a knock at the front door. Two raps, a pause, then three more. Kilo leapt up, shuffled through the doorway; he didn't bark but stood, tail wagging, in the middle of the living room.

"Doorbell's still broken?" Francine said.

Wells stepped out of the kitchen, around Kilo. He opened the front door just wide enough to see out. A man stood on the porch — short and slight, wearing a light jacket and a golf cap that he took off as the door opened. His pale, reddish hair was thin on top, and messy, his unblinking blue eyes set close together. He held a parcel wrapped in brown paper under one arm.

"Good evening," he said. "Hello."

"I'm sorry. We don't — "

"I'm a friend." The man put his hand on the door, lightly, as if to keep it from being closed. "A friend of Francine?" He stepped past Wells, gently forcing his way inside. "Hello, I'm dreaming."

Francine stood in the doorway to the kitchen. It seemed she could come no closer; she looked at the man as he gazed back in silence. He smiled, let his expression settle to neutral, then smiled again. There was a gap, where he was missing a tooth. The whiskers on his throat grew much more thickly than those on his face.

"Francine?" Wells said.

"We're friends," the man said.

"We knew each other a long time ago," Francine said. "When we were children. This is Colville. Colville Young. And this is my husband, Wells."

Colville didn't seem to see the hand Wells held out. Instead, he set his parcel on the floor, reached down to scratch Kilo's back.

"Some kind of Labrador?"

"Some kind," Francine said. "Mixed with something smaller."

Wells wondered if he should close the door, how long the man planned to stay. The living room felt crowded. From the kitchen, a commercial for Caldwell Subaru and Mazda blared; he was about to go turn the radio off just as Colville spoke again.

"You're taller than I am, Francine."

"I was always taller," she said.

"You're expecting a child."

"Yes," she said. "Soon. I guess you can see that."

"Here." He picked up the parcel, stepped closer, handed it to her, then stepped back again. "I brought this for you. Books, is all. They might be helpful." Watching her, he took off his hat with a twisting motion, jammed it in his jacket pocket. "Sometimes," he said. "Sometimes, Francine, I think of that day when you fell out of the tree. You remember that?"

"When was this?" Wells said.

"You fell from the top." Colville looked to the ceiling, slowly brought his gaze to the floor. "Forty, fifty feet, and you weren't hurt at all. You were being looked after, that day —"

"I remember," Francine said. "I was lucky."

"I've been thinking of you." Colville glanced through the doorway, into the kitchen. "I forgot it was dinnertime. I just wanted to come when you might be home — I know I could've called, but phones, phones aren't the same. It's just that I've been thinking of you, Francine. But now it's dinnertime."

"We've eaten," she said. "Here, would you like to sit down? Something to drink?"

"Orange juice," he said. "Or water would be fine."

Wells watched Francine go into the kitchen, still carrying the wrapped parcel, Kilo following. "So," he said, "what brings you to Boise?"

"I was up in Spokane, so it wasn't really too far." Colville took off his jacket, set it on the back of the chair. Sitting down, he faced Wells without really looking at him. He wore a purple T-shirt and beige dress pants, pointed black boots that zipped up the inside. The instep of the left one was patched with duct tape.

The sound of the radio in the kitchen was suddenly gone, switched off.

13

"I noticed the trucks outside," he said. "In front of your house."

"A girl disappeared," Wells said. "She lived down the street. She was sleeping in her back yard."

"Did you see all the blue ribbons in the trees?" Francine said, returning from the kitchen. She handed Colville a glass of orange juice, set her tea on the coffee table. "Blue was her favorite color. We've been searching."

Turning in his chair, Colville reached into the pocket of his jacket and took out a folded piece of newspaper. When he'd unfolded it, he held it out to them. It was a picture of the lost girl's face, an article about her disappearance.

"I'm searching, too," he said. "I have a feeling that I'm going to find her, that I'm the one." His voice was soft; his statements sounded more like questions. His head and upper body seemed calm, relaxed, but his feet kept twitching. He crossed his legs, uncrossed them, crossed them the other way.

"No luck yet, I guess," Wells said, but Colville didn't seem to hear him. He was staring at Francine, speaking to her.

"Has it been fifteen years?" he said. "Almost twenty, since we've been together? I've been thinking of that, how strange it is. It never seemed possible we'd be apart so long."

"You look older," she said. "That's good, I think. It makes sense, I mean. Are you growing a beard?"

"Or gotten lazy." Colville rubbed his cheeks. "Comes in better on this one side than the other."

"Fifteen years," Wells said; he felt as if he were interrupting. "That's a long time."

"And how long have the two of you been married?"

"Just over a year."

"I imagine Francine's probably mentioned me, then." Colville smiled, his tongue pressing against the gap in his teeth. "People in the Activity joked about how we were going to get married, the way we were always together."

"Were you going out?" Wells said.

"Pardon me?"

"Were you boyfriend and girlfriend?"

"We were too young," Francine said. "It was much different than that."

"People used to think we were brother and sister," Colville said. "On account of our hair and everything, how we lived together."

"Our families shared a trailer," Francine said, "for a little while."

"Until the Messenger called my family down to Corwin Springs." Colville now turned toward Wells. "My father was an electrician, so they needed him to work on the big shelter there. And then the Messenger wanted my mom near the Heart, while she was pregnant with my brother, closer to the energy, there."

"The Heart?" Wells said.

"It was a place," Francine said.

"It is a place," Colville said.

"Are you hungry?" she said. "Did I ask you that?"

"No," Colville said. "Yes, I mean. I've eaten, but you didn't ask me. Thank you for asking."

Francine began talking about college in Utah, how she'd met Wells there—she didn't mention that she'd graduated and he had not—and how they'd come here to Boise a year ago. She told about her job as a physician's assistant, how Wells worked at Home Depot. All the while, Colville stared at Francine with his eyes unfocused, gently shaking his head as if amazed to be in the same room with her. He looked away only when Kilo appeared from the hallway, claws tapping the wood floor, tail slapping the air. The dog turned two circles, leaned against Colville's legs, and looked up, whining to have his ears scratched.

"Likes you," Wells said. "That's unusual, with strangers."

"I got this real thing with animals lately. Almost like my brother, the way he did."

"Moses?" Francine said.

"All the dogs and cats used to gather outside our trailer when he was sleeping," Colville said. "And then he'd go outside and he'd be this little boy with all these pets behind him, following everywhere. Even birds would be flying tree to tree, trying to keep up. Squirrels, too."

"Who's this?" Wells said.

"Colville's little brother," Francine said. "Their mom was pregnant when my folks passed away, when Maya and I went to live with our grandparents."

"I forget sometimes that you never met him," Colville said.

"Where is he now?"

"You haven't heard, then." Colville scratched Kilo's head, looking at the dog as he spoke. "There's no way you would've heard, I guess. He was over in Iraq, with the Marines, then back to Afghanistan, just this past spring. It was a roadside bomb, they said."

"I'm sorry."

"Animals sure liked him," Colville said. "Everyone remembers that."

In the silence, Wells wondered if he should stand up, turn on another lamp. The room was dim, which made it difficult to read expressions; sitting next to Francine, he could only see the side of her face. He could not catch her eye, guess what she was thinking. He shifted a little, but she was looking down at her feet, her mouth set in a smile he couldn't understand.

"Would you mind if I told you the story of how I came to be here?" Colville closed his eyes for a moment, bowed his head, then looked up, smiling first at Francine, then at Wells. "This has been over the last few weeks. I mean, not that I didn't think of you before, Francine. But I was living in Spokane, in a little garage, kind of converted into a house. I had a yard, and I'd get animals coming right through sometimes."

Turning his head, he gestured at the window, where dusk had turned to darkness, the glass reflecting back. "Anyway, one night I was awakened by a scratching. On the ceiling, the rooftop. A scrabbling, and then it was gone. In the morning I saw the prints, outside in the mud. There were scratches along the windowsill, too, like something had tried to peek inside, had watched me while I was sleeping."

Colville was almost whispering now. Francine listened intently, leaning forward with her eyes closed.

"The tracks were all wrecked by the rain, and I couldn't decide if it had four toes on its front feet, five on its back—and then I couldn't remember if rodents had five and five or even which animals were rodents." He laughed. "My father taught me all that, and I couldn't remember. But each night after that, when I got home from work I'd move my little card table close to the window, and I'd wait there, doing my crosswords and Sudokus, until I could feel something watching me. The first time I looked up, nothing was there. Only the window."

Colville suddenly stopped talking. He cocked his head, listening.

"What is it?" Francine said.

"Is there anyone else in the house?"

"No," she said. "Just us."

"Do you have a washroom I could use?"

"Down the hall there, between the two bedrooms." She pointed to the doorway, and Colville nodded. He rose, and Kilo followed close behind him.

Francine picked up her teacup, set it down. She looked tired, her hair pulled back in a loose ponytail, her lips moving slightly; Wells knew that this meant she was thinking, not that she was about to speak.

"Do you need something?" he said. "I'll get up."

"No," she said.

"Are we going to let him stay here?" He kept his voice low.

"What?"

"That's what this is about, has to be."

"I don't think that's what this is about."

"Is he all right?"

"I think so," she said.

Wells wanted to say more, but he kept expecting Colville to return. He strained to hear, wondering how long it had been. Had the man gone into their bedroom? Or downstairs?

"Francine," Colville said, coming in behind them, through the kitchen door. "It's so nice to see that picture of your folks there. At work on their shelter. Lifesavers."

"That was the name of the shelter," Francine said before Wells asked. "Because it was round."

"How's Maya?" Colville said. "I saw her there in the picture, too."

"Good. She moved back to Montana, lives in Bozeman."

"Family?"

"No," Francine said. "She lives alone."

Colville had not sat down in the chair again. Instead, he put on his jacket, zipped it up, gathered his cap in his hands.

"Are you going?" Francine said.

"Going?" He looked around the room, at the front door, behind him, then sat down. "It's nice to be here with you," he said.

"It's a surprise."

"You thought I forgot," he said. "Didn't you?"

"What?" she said.

"You thought I forgot where I was." He wiped at his lips, smiled.

"No," she said. "I didn't think that."

"In my story, I mean. I didn't forget."

"Okay."

Colville tilted his head toward the ceiling, then lowered his gaze slowly, his eyes half closed as he began to speak. "I'd sit there at night by the window, doing my puzzles, waiting for her. What I learned was to watch out of the corner of my eye, my peripheral vision, not to turn my head." He touched the edge of his eye with his fingertip. "And then the night came when I saw her — her sharp ears, and those thick hairs all around her bandit face. She'd sit on the sill and look in the window, like she wanted to help me somehow. If I stood up, she'd leap down, slip away. It looked more like she was climbing the ground, not running across it."

"A raccoon," Wells said.

"She was and she wasn't. Or she was more than that, too. What it was was the way she kept coming back—"

"You fed her?"

"I tried—marshmallows, tuna fish—but that wasn't what she was after." Colville checked Francine's face, to be certain she was following. "All that sitting there together, so close like that without talking—she came to remind me of you, Francine. And then I started to think of the raccoon as you. I came to believe, to see how it might be you, calling on me."

Francine lifted her hands, then set them down on her thighs again.

"It was you, wasn't it?"

"The raccoon?" she said.

"It wasn't just the raccoon," he said. "I should tell you that. The raccoon showed me that you were trying to reach me, but it was the girl who told me where you were."

"The girl?"

"The lost girl," he said. "Your neighbor girl."

"She told you?"

"I was reading the newspaper," Colville said, holding up his hands, trying to slow down. "When I was in Spokane, and I read about this girl. All at once, when I saw her picture, I knew I had to come find her. I had a feeling. And then, then on the first day I was out searching, who should I see but you—right after those weeks of the raccoon. So that's how I know that none of this is some sort of coincidence." He glanced at Francine. "And of course we were taught never to believe in coincidences."

"Let's just slow down for a minute," Wells said. "Hold on—"

"I did it," Colville said, suddenly standing. He spoke as if scolding himself. "I kept talking and now I went too far. I can feel it, I can see that now." He began patting his pockets, glancing around as if he might have dropped something.

"Wait," Francine said.

"I really have to go. I do. Thank you so much. I apologize." Turning, Colville pulled the door open, glanced back once. "Good night."

The door closed, and Wells and Francine sat for a moment; the sound of footsteps faded away outside.

"There he goes," Wells said.

"Colville."

"Was he always like that?"

"I guess. I don't know. He was a boy when I knew him. A long time ago."

Wells reached out, took Francine's hand.

"He seemed so nervous," she said, "or something."

"Or something," he said. "I could tell it bothered you."

"It was just such a surprise," she said. "After so long."

"And then all that about the raccoon," he said. "What was that about?"

"I don't know," she said, taking her hand back. "Nothing."

"And the newspaper article? What was up with that?"

"I have to work early," she said, standing. "I should take a bath."

Wells sat by himself for a moment, then went into the kitchen and wiped the crumbs from the table. He began loading the dishwasher. The air felt tight, as if the atmosphere were still settling. It had been only an hour since he opened the door and Colville stepped inside, started talking, tightening everything up.

Kilo scratched at the door. When had he gone out? Turning off the faucet, Wells let the dog in, then walked past the sink, down the hallway. The water was running in the bathtub, the sound echoing. He pushed the door open.

Francine sat on the edge of the tub in her underwear and her shirt, pulling off one of her socks. Her belly made it hard for her to reach, to bend over. Standing, she began to pull off her shirt, then paused and looked at him, as if surprised to see that he was still there.

"Did he really think you turned into a raccoon?" he said.

"No," she said. "I don't think that's what he meant."

"That's how it sounded."

"If you grew up like we did, it might make more sense."

"I didn't," he said. "And I doubt it would make more sense."

Wells stepped closer; he reached out and traced the dark line that ran from her navel to the wide elastic of her underwear. It surprised him how hard her stomach was, how taut. He expected a ripple, a kick, but nothing came.

"Linea negra," she said.

"What?"

"Black line," she said. "That's what they call it."

He wiped condensation from the mirror. "You don't have to stop undressing."

"We're talking," she said.

"Do you think we'll see him again?"

"I have no idea," she said, turning away. "Would you close the door when you go out, so the cold air doesn't come in?"

3

TWO DAYS PASSED, three. Francine had been working for most of them — leaving early, coming home late. Tonight Wells lay in bed, listening until he heard her car in the driveway, her key in the door.

Kilo leapt from the bed and rushed down the hall; he returned in a moment, leading Francine into the bedroom.

"You didn't have to wait up," she said.

"I wanted to."

She shrugged her shoulders and let her white coat fall to the wooden floor with a heavy, dull clatter. A notebook came free and the rubber tube of a stethoscope slapped out, its metal bell bouncing.

"It's just the weight of it all," she said. "The coat, the baby, everything." She took out her earrings, set them on her dresser, then picked up something else.

"What's that?" he said.

"A heart," she said, holding it out to show him. "A wooden heart." It fit in the palm of her hand.

"I've never seen it before."

"It's nothing — I've had it a long time, since I was a girl."

Francine went down the hallway again. He heard water running in the bathroom and then the sound of her sighing. He waited.

When she returned, he switched off the lamp on the bedside table; he held the blankets up, so she could slide underneath, press her back against him. Pulling down the straps of her nightgown, he ran his thumbs along the sharp ridges of her shoulder blades, his fingers up under her hair, along her neck.

"That's better," she said.

"Remember that time," he said, "on the way to Moab? What was the name of that town, that motel?"

"Beaver. The Beaver Inn. That was a good time."

Outside, a horn honked, a dog barked, and then it was silent again. The moonlight eased through a gap in the curtains; pale freckles spread across Francine's skin.

"I thought," he said, "before, when I was thinking of all this time before the baby came, that it would be just us, the two of us, you know, doing all the things we wouldn't be able to do for so long."

"If I don't work all these shifts now," she said, "I'll hardly have a maternity leave. You'll see a lot of me, then."

"But you won't be alone."

"Jealous?"

He laid his palms flat on the small of her back, pressing gently. Outside, the wind raced through the trees; the house creaked and settled.

"This reminds me of when I was a girl," she said. "How Maya and I used to talk in bed. We used to rub each other's back."

"You shared a bed?"

"It was a mattress on the floor of the living room."

"This was in the trailer?"

"On our side of the living room. The room was cut in half by a bookcase, where our altar was on one side and Colville's family's on the other."

"What kind of altar?"

"I've been thinking," she said. "Of how much fun we had back then. Playing around. Talking to Maya. Just being out in the canyons and everything." She rolled over, almost trapping his hands beneath her body, her face close to his, her belly firm against him. "Sometimes it's hard to figure out how I got from there to here."

"But you did," he said. "Here you are."

"Yes, I did," she said. "And I am here." She turned over, away from him once more; she was silent for a moment, and then she spoke again. "Having an older sister definitely helped. Maya had the answers. For the kids at school, I mean. Once we were in Seattle, living with our grandparents, she told me how to answer the questions: 'Of course our parents had guns — didn't everyone hunt?' 'Well, in Switzerland everyone's required to have a bomb shelter.' And most of my friends' parents were hippies, so if anyone asked about our church we could talk about Buddhism, or Taoism or Confucius. It didn't feel like I was lying — I was just figuring out how to tell my story so I could fit in."

"Did it work?"

"I don't know," she said. "We tried. It wasn't like we could go to Methodist church with our grandparents, that that made sense. We were used to being surrounded by people who all believed the same, who were preparing for the same things, you know? So when we moved away, we lost all that. It was hard to know what to do."

"And you lost your folks, too."

"That's what I'm saying." Francine shifted, straightened her legs. "Knowing we're going to have the baby makes me think about them, my parents. It makes me remember everything, how it was."

Wells waited. In the past she'd never wanted to talk about her childhood. She laughed it off or changed the subject; if he waited long enough, he hoped, the time would come when she would tell him about it.

"Seeing your friend, too," he said.

"What?"

"Seeing Colville makes you remember."

"Yes," she said.

"Have you seen him since the other night?"

"No. I figure he's gone back to Spokane or wherever."

"Spokane," he said, "where you're a raccoon."

"Whatever, Wells."

"I saw him," he said.

"Colville?"

"The last couple mornings I've seen him. Just walking up the street."

"Our street?" she said. "Why didn't you tell me?"

"You have enough to worry about."

Francine didn't say anything. The curtains shifted faint shadows along the ceiling. Kilo, in the kitchen, pushed his bowl across the linoleum, lapped water from his dish.

"He went to all the trouble to find you," Wells said. "There must be some reason."

"Maybe that was the reason."

"What?"

"Just to find me, to check up on me. I don't know."

"Creepy."

"To me, he just seemed lonely."

Francine reached back and pulled the blanket up over her shoulder, covering her ear. Her toes pressed down on the tops of his feet. Reaching for her hip, he rested his hand on her belly.

"I wonder where that girl is now," she said. "I wonder what her parents are doing."

"They're probably asleep."

"Right now?" she said. "With everything? They can't sleep."

"We're the ones who are awake."

Francine reached back, patted his leg. "Let's sleep now. Sleep."

"Do you think he knows anything about her?" Wells said. "Colville, I mean. He had that newspaper and everything. Maybe he knows something."

"He's probably just searching, like he said."

26

"So he saw the raccoon, then read the newspaper, and all of a sudden he's knocking on your door?"

"What are you saying?"

"Did you ever talk to anyone?" he said. "A reporter?"

"No."

"If your name was in that article," he said, "then he'd know where you were, where to find you."

"Wells," she said. "Colville wouldn't make it all up."

"How do you know?"

"I know him."

"You knew him." Wells rolled onto his back, stared up at the pale ceiling.

"People," she said, her voice drifting toward sleep. "People don't change that much."

◆

Wells awakened in the middle of the night, and Francine wasn't in bed. He lay still, listening. Beyond, through the cold wind in the trees, he heard a tapping. Not rain; something else.

He rolled over, checked the alarm clock: it was half past three. Pulling the covers aside, he stood and moved quietly into the hallway, careful where floorboards creaked. He went into the bathroom, the tile cold beneath his feet. The tapping was louder here. Francine was typing on the computer in the guest room, the room that would be the baby's.

He wondered if he should switch on the light, flush the toilet, so she would know he was awake and it wouldn't seem that he was sneaking around. Back in the hallway he moved closer, leaned his ear against the door. The doorknob rattled; the typing stopped.

"You're up?" she said.

"Only because you are," he said, the door still between them. "You okay?"

"Can't sleep."

"Come back to bed."

"It's better to do something than to lie awake," she said.

Wells leaned away from the door. He did not open it, did not put his hand on the knob and turn it.

"Are you still out there?" she said.

"Yes," he said.

"Why?"

"What is it?" he said. "Something at work?"

"Go to sleep," she said.

When he turned the knob and the door opened, Francine looked up, startled. The blue light of the computer screen glowed on the skin of her face, cast shadows in the folds of her bathrobe. Two books and some papers rested on the desk, next to the keyboard.

"What are you typing?"

"Nothing," she said, turning back to the screen. "Things for the baby. To be prepared, I guess."

"Are those the books Colville gave you?"

"Yes."

"What are they?"

"They're about babies, how to care for babies. That's all." She lifted them, held them up for him to see, then slid them away, into the shadows.

"How did he know?"

"He saw me out searching for the girl," she said. "He said that, remember? Why are you being so weird about him?"

"Maybe because he's so weird?"

Francine smiled. "Anyone who saw me out walking around those hills would know that I'm pregnant. I hope they would, anyway."

He stood there, halfway in the room. "You really feel all right?"

"You asked that. I'll see you in the morning."

He stepped back and closed the door, then stood still for a moment, waiting. He listened as the tapping resumed, then turned and walked down the hallway to the bedroom.

◆

In the morning he spread his arms wide, hands gripping the edges of the mattress. He stared at the ceiling, its hairline cracks visible in the half-light. The sheets on Francine's side felt tight, as if she'd made the bed around him. Had he heard her get into bed, or had she never returned?

It was now past seven. He pulled the covers aside, swung his legs around, put his bare feet on the cold floor. In the bathroom the tub was drained, dry, clean, the towels on the rack barely damp. He stepped over Francine's white cotton underwear on the floor, her maternity corduroys. Her toothbrush stuck up from the cup, its bristles still wet.

In the kitchen the dishwasher was open, the dishes clean but not put away. Francine's mug, her plate full of toast crumbs, rested in the sink. The morning looked cold, the sun just clearing the ridges.

He could see, down the hallway, that the door of the baby's room was ajar. He moved closer, touched it with his finger, pushed it a few inches further: the guest mattress propped against the wall, the new crib with its mobile of colored horses, the desk. Stepping inside, closer, he saw the books on the other side of the computer monitor. He unstacked them, spread them out so he could read the titles: *Nurturing Your Baby's Soul: A Spiritual Guide for Expectant Parents; Saint Germain, Master Alchemist;* and the third, more of a pamphlet, with a photo-copied cover of Mary and baby Jesus, its title in rough calligraphy: *The Science of Motherhood for the New Age.*

He shuffled through the pamphlet's pages — some dog-eared, underlined, ringed by old coffee cups. He stopped at a passage highlighted in yellow: *If you really follow this path, with all your*

29

heart, use the Violet Flame, use all the meditations and the proper diet — really pursue God — you can have control over your families. You can reach the place where souls of Light and great attainment are born to you. And by the science of the spoken Word and your own decrees, you can bring forth advanced souls with bodies and with genes that are adequate to their consciousness. The sacred fire in your heart determines what sort of soul you can magnetize to your temple.

Had Colville highlighted this passage for Francine, or had someone else done it, in another place, another time? Now Wells touched the words, imagined Francine reading about souls and magnetism and consciousness. Would she laugh? Would this all seem somehow familiar?

4

IT WAS LATE AFTERNOON and Wells sat in the living room, watching the street through the window. Waiting. He'd gotten off work early, the last few days; he was trying to figure out what Colville was doing.

And here the man came, walking quickly, not even glancing at the house. The way he walked — he lifted his feet higher than was necessary, his spine rigidly straight despite the heavy frame pack he wore.

Wells went out the side door, onto the driveway, then into his truck. He drove slowly, staying a half block back. The orange pack made the following easier. He knew where Colville was going — first to Jackson's, to pick up some food, and then to some motel, where he'd get a room. Wells had learned, in the last few days, that Colville shuttled between motels; he'd stay two or three nights in a place, or sometimes only one. He'd double back, sleep one place on Monday, someplace else on Tuesday and Wednesday, then return to the first place again on Thursday.

Today was Friday, and Colville came out of the store with a bunch of bananas in his hand. He ate them as he walked, that orange pack bobbing along, swaying slightly from side to side. Wells shifted back into gear, eased out into traffic. When he got too close, he pulled over, waited, then resumed his pursuit. If Colville saw him, that would be fine. Perhaps today was the day they'd talk; perhaps Colville knew he was here right now.

At the Econo Lodge, Wells parked on the street, where he

could watch the office that Colville had entered. He could also see the narrow parking lot, the low wall that shielded the pool from sight. The doors' brass numbers glinted in the cold sun. No one opened the doors, or the curtains in the windows; no one stood on the balcony except a maid moving her cart of fresh towels and sheets slowly along.

Five minutes passed, and then Colville reappeared. Fifty feet away, carrying a small blue bucket in one hand, walking in front of the white wall so his shadow slid next to him like a tilting companion.

Wells opened the door of his truck and started across the parking lot, almost tripping on the curb.

Colville glanced up. "I thought that was you over there, Wells."

"I wanted to talk to you."

Colville smiled. "We're talking." He was so skinny. He wore a black sweater with holes in the elbows; his pants were actually coveralls, the arms tied off around his waist. The square top of the pack framed his face with orange, tinting his skin.

"I've seen you," Wells said. "Walking past our house in the morning, coming back the other way in the afternoon."

"Probably so," Colville said. "I suspect I do."

"I'm asking you to stop it. That's all I'm asking." Wells tried to keep his voice down. "Francine doesn't need you hanging around like that."

Colville laughed. "I see," he said. "I understand how that might look now. But you've misunderstood things. I'm here to find the girl, like I told you. Or that's why I came here. That's what I'm doing, though Francine being here can't be a coincidence."

"I'm asking you to stop. How you think I understand things doesn't matter."

"Francine and I," Colville said. "You couldn't really understand where we're from, the path we started on. She's my oldest friend —"

"But that was a long time ago," Wells said. "Things are different now. You're different people."

"We're not so different." Colville held up his hands, palms facing out. "I like you, Wells," he said, his voice soft. "It's so fine that Francine's with a person like you, looking out for her, trying to protect her. We have to help her in every way we can."

Turning away, he began to walk toward the motel. Wells followed; at first he rushed, but then he tried to slow down, to calm himself.

"What I'm saying," he said, "is that we don't need your help. We don't want to see you outside our house."

Colville now stood in the shade of the motel, facing Wells. He set his ice bucket on the roof of a parked car, then swung his pack around, leaned it there. He untied the sleeves of his coveralls and pulled the whole thing up over his shoulders, the sleeves going straight and his hands appearing at the cuffs.

"I understand how it is," he said. "You might see me pass in the morning and then again in the afternoon. And all day you're in those tall aisles at the Home Depot, wearing your orange vest, answering questions, finding things for people, and you're wondering if I'm outside your house, trying to get someone's attention, looking in your windows and over your fence, getting your dog riled up. But that's not how it is."

The car Colville leaned against was an old blue station wagon, half its plastic wood paneling torn off. A tattered dream-catcher hung from the rearview mirror; the seats were folded down flat in back. Colville rubbed at the side mirror with a finger as he talked, and Wells tried to look past him, into the car, to see what it held. A rolled-up camouflage sleeping bag, an empty birdcage, a half-deflated soccer ball, a tangle of wire.

"It's true," Colville said. "I do pass by your house, but what it is is that your house just happens to be on my way to where I'm headed, when I'm searching for your neighbor girl. I'll simply take another route if it's bothering you. Believe me, I have nothing to hide from you, I'm not trying to hide anything, but I don't understand it all yet myself, everything that's happening, or why. I do believe it'll all make sense eventually—"

A voice interrupted him, shouting from the balcony above. A red-faced man in a white dress shirt and tie was pointing down at them.

"That's my car! Don't lean on it!"

"No harm, no harm," Colville said, picking up his ice bucket. He pretended to polish the car with the cuff of his sleeve, where he had touched it.

"You want me to lean on your car?" the man said. "What are you thinking?"

"I don't have a car," Colville said.

"And that was you last night, wasn't it? All that singing?"

"Pardon me?" Colville said.

"You think I can't hear that, through the floor?"

"I apologize for leaning on your car." Colville tipped his bucket to spill the melted water on the asphalt, then peered into it as if disappointed with the amount of ice that remained. He lifted his pack to one shoulder as he moved under the balcony, out of the man's view.

"I'll stop walking past your house, Wells," he said, his voice lower. "I have some things to do now."

Stepping to a door with a brass 12 on it, he fit the key into the lock, turned it. He went in without looking back and closed the door quickly behind him, as if he didn't want anyone to see inside.

Wells drove away, toward home. He called Francine's cell and it went straight to voicemail; he didn't leave a message. He hoped she was waiting at home, awake, though he couldn't blame her for sleeping, considering the hours she'd been working.

As he turned into the driveway, he saw the girl. She coasted down the sidewalk on that red bike, dark hair blowing behind her. She swooped past, circled around as he parked the truck and climbed out.

"Hello," he said.

"Hi," she said, slowing but not stopping.

"I live right here," he said. "It's okay. I'm your neighbor."

"I know that," she said.

"Your name's Della?" he said.

"Everyone knows that!" Standing up on her pedals, she sped away, looking back over her shoulder as she reached her blue house, where a shadow shifted in an upstairs window. Her mother or father, keeping track. Lately they'd been on the radio, asking for help, pleading with whoever had taken their daughter to come forward, to bring her back. There was a new billboard of her giant face, too, that hung over the highway, looking down at him as he drove to work.

Wells walked around the truck, unlatched the gate to the back yard, let Kilo out. The dog followed him in through the side door, into the kitchen. Down the hallway, Wells eased the bedroom door open, squinted in the dim light. The bed was made, or half made, as he'd left it this morning.

"Francine?" he called, just raising his voice.

He'd forgotten — she'd said something about picking up an extra shift, perhaps, working tonight. Something like that. He walked back into the kitchen, looked out the window. Francine's car wasn't in the driveway — he hadn't even noticed on the way in. He picked up the phone on the counter, dialed her cell again.

"Kilo," he said, stumbling. "You're underfoot."

As he waited for Francine to answer, or to leave a message, the ringing in his ear was echoed by a louder ringing somewhere in the house. He followed the sound down the hallway to the bedroom, where Francine's phone was ringing atop her bare dresser. He almost answered it, then hung up the other phone, still in his hand. The house went quiet again.

The baby's room had become Francine's place, where she went

in the middle of the night, typing on the computer or rearranging the baby's things. He stepped inside – the crib, the mobile, the desk – and opened the closet, looked at the metal shelves they'd installed there months before. Baby clothes and blankets, all shades of blue and purple, all chosen by Francine. He lifted up a fleece sleep suit, set it down. What if they had a girl?

The computer hummed, the screensaver bouncing a prism of colored light from edge to edge. When he tapped the keyboard, the screen flashed blue and, after a moment, began cycling through pictures of other times, other places. Back on the campus in Salt Lake City, not long after they met; and when Kilo was a puppy; a photo of himself, swimming in a mountain lake last summer; then one of Francine, just the long pale length of her, running across a campsite, smiling, right before she ran off into the forest like that. It was gone too quickly, shifting to a picnic, then a picture of this house when they bought it, the rooms so bare –

Wells stood watching, forgetting everything, laughing to himself with each new picture, and then the screen dimmed and went black again, reflecting his expectant face, his hair sticking up, his arms crossed. He stepped back, looked around. The mattress leaning against the wall, the desk, the closed closet door, the wheeled office chair with dust on its vinyl arms. Above the crib, the horses on the mobile spun, the air stirred by his body moving inside this space.

When he tapped the space bar on the keyboard, the screensaver stopped, and the photos started again. He tapped the space bar again and then the screen shone bright blue. He clicked on the hard drive, then the Documents folder, checked the dates when files had last been edited.

In the silence he expected to hear the door opening, Francine's voice calling his name. He clicked on the document named "Shelter Cycle," then waited, the white rectangle opening.

The page was full of words, sentences, paragraphs. He read the first line:

> When I was out by myself in the mountains, I liked to think he was somewhere in the trees.

His gaze trailed down, skipping ahead. He reached for the chair, began to sit, then switched on the printer, checked the tray. He'd print it all out, then read it in the living room — that way he could see Francine returning, if she wasn't working tonight, if she came home early.

For the big services and the conferences we drove south from Glastonbury, along the Yellowstone River, twenty or so miles to Corwin Springs, where the headquarters were and the Messenger lived.

This was in our station wagon, my father driving and my mother leading the Archangel Michael decrees, for protection. Maya and I sat in the back; behind us and in front of us drove other cars from the Activity, our combined energy keeping Entities and Forcefields at bay. If a motorcycle passed, we sped up our decrees, got louder. No person with any Light rode a motorcycle, only Fallen Ones who liked the vibration between their legs, the noise and the smoke. You had to be careful not to let such a rider look into your eyes.

If it was summer we went up into the mountains, to a high meadow full of energy, the Heart of the Inner Retreat. In the winter the services happened in a big building, a chapel called King Arthur's Court; it only held the adults, so we children were split up by age and taken to trailers, where we were fed and could sleep until our parents were finished.

This night that's where we were, in a trailer. The women called to tend us bustled around the kitchen, where all the cabinets and doors had to be completely shut at all times, to keep dark spirits from getting in or coming out. Above the door that went outside was a picture of Cyclopea, the all-seeing eye of God. A right eye, blue, with rays shooting out. It never stopped watching us.

Colville lived here, at Corwin Springs; he'd moved away from us months before. His hair hung down in his eyes so he was always shaking his head now, and he had new friends. He didn't sit with me. He sat right behind me, his back almost touching mine, so I could hear him talking.

I could tell by my feelings that I missed him, his family, all the space where his family had been; we hadn't moved into their rooms. I ate my rice-and-bean stew and listened as he talked about the shelter up at the Heart, how his father had shown it to him even though he wasn't supposed to. The shelter would hold more than seven hundred people, and there was another underground place for animals. We'd need animals after the blast, ones that hadn't breathed fallout or radiation. There were also storage rooms full of coins, since paper money wouldn't be any good, and a concrete vault where all the Messenger's Teachings and dictations would be kept. There were even places, Colville said, where army tanks were hidden, ready to protect us.

The trailer was crowded. Kids cried, some talking in a language no one understood. Some of the adults tried Spanish, and that didn't work. They decided the kids were Dutch. No one spoke that.

After they took our plates away, the adults wheeled a television out on a cart. The service was broadcast on a closed circuit from King Arthur's Court, and the adults wanted to watch it. They told us to play quietly with the jigsaw puzzles and the geography books. We half obeyed, whispering to each other, looking sideways at the screen. At first there was only silence; people filed in, sitting in a special order. They meditated with their hands on their knees, their palms facing upward. The altar had a huge picture of Saint Germain and one of Jesus Christ; between them was a bigger picture of the Chart of Your Divine Self, all blue and purple and white rays, the little person at the bottom with the Crystal Cord reaching up from his heart, up to ascension. Below that was a long golden table covered in flowers. Soon the people on the screen began to decree.

> *I AM the Violet Flame*
> *In action in me now*
> *I AM the Violet Flame*
> *To Light alone I bow*

Along the trailer's floor, mats had been rolled out for us. As the decrees came in their rhythm, over and over, they lulled us all toward sleep. Colville lay on a mat near mine, stretched out on his stomach, drawing something on a piece of paper, whispering to himself. I was working on a puzzle of three puppies, black and white, playing in some flowers. On the screen the whole crowd was decreeing. I could hear it outside, too, from other trailers and maybe even from King Arthur's Court, half a mile away. *Hail Saint Germain! Hail Saint Germain! Hail Saint Germain!* They raised their hands and chanted louder.

> *I AM the Violet Flame*
> *In mighty Cosmic Power*
> *I AM the Violet Flame*
> *Shining Every Hour*
> *I AM the Violet Flame*
> *Blazing like a sun*
> *I AM God's sacred power*
> *Freeing everyone*

The decree came fast, in circles. With every time around, the energy rose. The more voices, the more vibration, the more Light to send out into the world. The Violet Flame decrees shook the bad thoughts and feelings from us, and situations, and other people, far away. If our thoughts vibrated with enough power, we could see and understand things that had been beyond our range before, like the way dogs can hear whistles at high frequencies. If we could balance the dark with our Light, so much more would be visible. For instance, all the Elementals that surrounded us.

I slowly slid my mat closer to the television. I leaned in toward the screen and stared into all the tiny decreeing faces, listened to their voices. Sometimes in a service, the Light would come down so powerfully that a person would just collapse. I could see that happening, here and there in the crowd, and I leaned close, squinting to be sure it wasn't my mom. I was always afraid that she would be taken by the spirit. My father, he loved to decree. Once I heard him say that decreeing surrounded by hundreds of people for twelve hours straight was better than putting two hits of acid on his tongue. What he meant was that it took his soul out of his body, happy, closer to where we all came from.

Someone whispered my name, then. It was Colville, still flat on his stomach, sliding closer. He whispered, his voice along the floor, telling me that the two of us were not supposed to be apart, but that we had to be, for a time, because of his brother. He said that the Messenger had been talking with his brother, even though the baby wasn't born yet. The baby would be special, a boy of great Light, necessary in the coming trials. I nodded. I told him I believed it, and I did believe it. We both went silent, watching and listening, so close together again.

All the decreeing had finally cleared enough energy that the Messenger could appear. She entered the stage in a white gown, floating almost, sitting on a blue chair while things settled. Then she stood and crossed the blue stage, flowers all around, crystal chandeliers overhead. There was no sound at all until she spoke.

She called everyone dearly beloved friends, Keepers of the Flame. She warned that not enough Violet Flame had yet been called forth to reverse the tide, to transmute or stop her prophecies from coming into being. Her voice echoed. She said that she had been on Atlantis and Lemuria and that she was still here, loving us. Her face was fixed, staring; and then her voice went deeper, into a kind of monotone, as she dictated from the Ascended Master Saint Germain. His handsome face shone in the painting behind her – his blond mustache and pointed beard and swept-back hair, his calm, pale eyes.

Through the Messenger he told us that we should stay close to the shelters, to listen to the news. He seemed to be promising something, to know something, and not quite to say it to us. He told us to give up earthly attachments, to be willing to leave everything behind.

The Ascended Masters could speak to us only through the Messenger. She spoke in their voices, dictated their thoughts and feelings with her voice. When the Masters communicated, it was at such a high vibration that only the Messenger could hear them. And even if you could hear or see a Master, your body would be shaken apart by the energy, the vibrations. The Messenger could withstand it, so their voices came through her to us.

Some of this, as I write it now, hardly seems real to me, or believable. But I wonder how much anything can slip away from inside you if you believed it at one time. I write one memory in this letter, then remember another, and another, all coming up from inside to surprise me.

That night I closed my eyes because it hurt them to stay focused on the Messenger too long. I smelled propane, heard the baseboard heaters' rattle. I wasn't afraid. I trusted my parents, even if our shelter held only seventy people, not seven hundred. I knew we were prepared. Stretched out, I listened, the puzzle pieces close to my face, the smell of cardboard.

The Ascended Masters were once people like us who had simply shone a little brighter, a brotherhood of spiritual beings who had ascended. Instead of staying in the higher planes, they came back to work with us, to make life on earth better. There were hundreds of them, and they all had different concerns, and we had to learn from each of them. The ones we mostly talked about were the Masters of the Seven Rays, the colors of the visible spectrum. Saint Germain was on the seventh ray, the Violet Ray, and violet light had the shortest wavelength, the highest frequency, the most energy, the greatest ability to change matter. He had been in Atlantis as well as Lemuria, like the Messenger, and in his embodiments he'd lived as the prophet Samuel, and Joseph, Christopher Columbus, Merlin the Magician, Francis Bacon, and plenty of others. His ray was also called the Freedom Ray, which is what made him so interested in America.

The Masters watched everything we did, and they would tell the Messenger. How much meat we ate, or if we wore red or black or had it in our house. If we listened to rock and roll, if we decreed or did not decree. If our Light was shining or if it was dim.

While we children slept in that trailer, the dictations, the decrees, the voices entered us, our dreams, taught us. I don't know if I slept. When I looked up again, the Messenger was still talking, now swinging a large sword through the air, slicing through the energy, piercing the planes where dark Entities lurked, waiting to do us wrong. I'd taken my shoes off, or someone else had; I stood, barefoot, and wove my way unsteadily around all the other kids, asleep on the floor. The adults were still watching the screen, whispering decrees. They didn't notice me.

I went into the bathroom and shut the door. I did not turn on the light. The one window was iced, frosted over, and when I turned the handle the ice cracked and the window came open, a little at a time. Cold air sliced in; I was awake.

The snow had stopped falling. Squares of yellow glowed, the windows of other trailers, where people were still listening to the service. Moonlight shone down on the white slopes.

The Messenger's voice was everywhere, traveling all through that lighted landscape. I couldn't make out the words she was saying. It felt special that thousands of other people were so quiet, listening between the words, listening to the words. There was this wonderful hush of attention, this echoing voice that everyone in all the miles around us was straining to hear, that was focusing us all in this amazing way. All up the white slopes into the dark trees, the night sky, the canyons where the narrow roads went, five miles away into the Heart of the Inner Retreat, where the shelter was waiting, where men were probably working at that very moment.

Later, much later, our parents came for us. They picked us up, bundled us up, carried us out to our idling cars with the heaters blasting. It had to be hours after midnight, and my parents didn't seem tired at all. They were energized, full of energy. I could feel the wild vibrations in their arms. The air around us felt like everything was about to happen.

5

A CANDLE, A MATCH. These were what Colville needed, and he was only half unpacked; he'd moved into this motel room hours ago, and tomorrow he'd be gone again. It was a precaution, this constant movement — it kept the dark forces and spirits confused, so they could not find and surprise him. After all, the Messenger herself had often slept in a golden bus that was driven all night, never still.

He felt so much inside these days, so much Light, as if anything were possible. There were still moments when he tried to explain something and people's expressions showed that they couldn't follow, or that they felt sorry for him — when he feared he would begin to cry, or he did start crying, just walking down the street or riding a bus. Those moments came less and less frequently now, the more he trusted his path, the further he followed it.

At last he found a book of matches in a drawer, a candle in the side pocket of his orange frame pack. After lighting the candle, he set it on the seat of the chair. He sat cross-legged on the floor and, placing his hand over his heart, stared at the flame for several seconds. He closed his eyes, visualized the flame in his mind's eye, turned it violet, held it there. It climbed, its point sharp; gradually, it began to flicker. He tried to draw his focus to his heart again, to slow his breathing. Yesterday, the flame had not wavered at all. He'd been so certain, he'd sensed that he was being called to the mountains, back to the Heart to renew his balance and purify his Light. Now he could not hold it steady. The violet flame forked and twisted.

A knock, a knocking at the door.

He opened his eyes.

He blew out the candle and steadied himself against the wall, then hurried to the door, squinted through the peephole.

Francine. Standing there, she licked her lips, turned her head from side to side.

"Hold on," he said. "Don't go." He found his pants on the floor, pulled them on, searched his pack for a clean shirt. Then, ready, he opened the door.

She wore white clogs, a white jacket with her name embroidered in red thread above the pocket. Cursive. Her hair was loose, sticking up a little on one side, and her dark eyes were on him, watching and waiting.

"Come in." He stepped aside. "Here."

"I tried to come, before," she said. "I got your message at work, but you weren't at the motel when I got there. It was a different motel."

"Sit down," he said, closing the door. "There, at the table. Please." He rolled up the yoga mat, set it out of the way, then settled on the chair across from her, with the table between them. Now that he was actually talking to her, he was less certain how to begin. He glanced up; the lines of her face were softer, her nose still straight and thin, her eyes drifting and then back in focus. She looked down at the table, up at him again. Her hand resting there was so close that he could reach out and touch it.

"Hi," she said, after a moment.

"Hi," he said.

"Are you nervous? You seem nervous."

"Not really," he said.

"I am. I don't know why."

The table hid her stomach — he couldn't see that she was pregnant, and yet he couldn't forget the fact of it, couldn't not feel it. Another person, inside her body and awaiting its soul, almost ready to come out to breathe air, to do all the things it would do.

"Sometimes," he said, "I hardly know what I'm going to say. So I try to slow down. The other night at your house, I could tell it was too much."

Voices, shadows passed on the other side of the curtained window. Headlights wheeled around the narrow motel parking lot. Colville waited for the voices to fade, for the cars to drive away.

"Did you read the books?" he said.

"I looked through them, a little, and it was interesting. Some of it. But most of it just seemed so far away from my life, now."

"I studied them before I gave them to you. I think they'll help, if you pay attention."

As he spoke, he felt her looking past him, at the candle on the chair, the white plastic cooler. The television, unplugged and turned to face the wall. In the shadowy mirror above the sink, at the back of the room, he could see her and himself, both sitting at the table in these chairs, not quite facing each other.

"I look so small," he said. "And my hair's almost gone. I must seem totally different to you."

Francine smiled as she looked to the window, the curtain, then back at him.

"What?" he said.

"I was thinking of you," she said. "Of back when we were kids. Even before you came to my house the other night, I mean. I was thinking of that broken cabin we played in, and how we put crystals in the little caves, for the Elementals."

"You see how it is?" he said. "You were thinking of me, and then the raccoon – "

"I'm not sure it works like that," she said. "But it's something about having the baby that reminds me of how it was, growing up, and my parents and everything – how it was back then. When you came to my house and we were talking, I was thinking how nice it was to not have to hide anything, not to have to explain everything."

"And still," he said, "that night, I felt maybe your husband, that you couldn't quite say what you wanted to tell me in front of him."

"I was just surprised," she said, "to have you suddenly there. I didn't expect it. He was surprised, too."

"I didn't warn you."

"No, you didn't."

"I saw him," Colville said, "your husband. I talked to him a little, just earlier today. He's a good person, I think. He's worried, and he doesn't want me to bother you, I guess, so he's been watching me." Colville glanced up; Francine nodded, listening. "Not that you can blame him," he said. "The way I showed up, the way I talked. It was fine — he's fine. It's not like he could really understand everything."

"He does worry," she said, after a moment.

Reaching back, Colville lifted the lid of the cooler beside the bed; he picked up a piece of ice, dropped it again, closed the lid.

"Do you remember," he said, "the time we ran circles, around and around the shelter?"

"We shot pieces of that pink insulation through the vacuum tubes," she said, laughing, "all the way from underground out into the sky."

"Then we ran outside and found them," he said. "And how about the periscope?"

"When we sneaked into the lookout room and spied on Maya walking past?"

"And her friend, too."

"Courtney," Francine said. "That was her friend's name. Courtney Stiller."

"I always thought," he said. "I see now how I always felt I'd know you — and then you moved away and I forgot, I tried to forget, but now it seems the same, like the time wasn't a problem, really, that we shouldn't worry, that it's like the Messenger said. We'll help each other."

Francine rested her hands flat on the table; she didn't interrupt.

"And you can't not feel it," he said. "You must feel it, the difference. You came here to meet me, after all."

"You kept leaving me those notes," she said. "I was curious."

"It had to be more than that — you must feel how everything's changing, how it's about to change."

"Of course." Francine laughed again, her hand on her belly. "Of course I feel different, of course things are changing. I've got all these hormones, I've got all sorts of preparations."

"Exactly," he said. "That's the Light, and the Teachings — the Messenger left so many behind."

"The Messenger's dead?"

"No," he said. "Yes. I mean, she's not the Messenger like she was." He pointed to the tape recorder, the line of cassette tapes on the dresser. "Just last night, I was listening to her — she was dictating from Saint Germain, all about the mountains, as the place where pilgrims go, holy mountains. That was really helpful."

"But she's alive," Francine said.

"In Bozeman," he said. "That's what I heard — at Murray Steinman's place. Her body's there; her soul, I don't know. The Alzheimer's, my folks said, but they could be wrong. They're not really involved in the Activity anymore. They drifted away from it, too, just like I did, just like you have."

"But you drifted back," she said. "Is that what you're saying?"

"I forgot," he said. "I tried to forget. I tried to believe other things, even. But then after Moses died, I started feeling the Light again." He grasped the wooden arms of his chair, slid it closer to the table, closer to her. "If you had seen me six months ago, you'd see how much happier I am now. Things are starting to make more sense again."

"I'm glad," she said. "I'm glad to hear that."

"It's hard," he said, "all the things they told us, to see how we could end up where we are, but we feel it again now. That's the important thing. I see how I was brought here to remind you, to help you prepare."

"I'm doing okay," she said. "I'm fine by myself—with Wells, I mean."

"Of course," Colville said. "That's not what I'm saying, not exactly. For now, I'm just reminding you. I have to go, in any case."

"Where?"

"Did I mention the mountains?" he said. "That's next, I believe."

"I thought you came here to find the girl."

"I thought that, too."

Francine leaned back, closed her eyes for a moment, rubbed at them.

"I should be home," she said. "It's late."

"Right," he said, standing. "You have to rest, that's right. You have to take care of yourself, of the soul that's coming."

But Francine didn't move, didn't get up to go. Colville sat down again.

"Think of your baby's soul," he said. "Waiting. Watching us right now, and all the time before, back in Glastonbury and you drifting away, meeting your husband, the two of you preparing a body for it, a new embodiment for the soul to take in this plane."

"The language," Francine said, laughing. "I'm sorry, the terminology, I mean. I would never remember it, but when you say it, it's so familiar—"

"See?" he said.

"I missed you," she said. "That night—"

"I missed you, too."

"I mean that first night," she said, "when I was in our shelter and you were down in the big shelter at the Heart, I missed you. I imagined you burrowing all the way to me, you know, digging for years. And then, when a hole opened up in my wall, you would tumble out, and you would be all grown up."

She laughed, and he laughed with her, both looking at their hands on the tabletop, their voices dwindling to silence.

"But isn't this the same," he said, "right now, how I found you? That's what you mean, right? I came back through all this time."

"It's just something I imagined."

Now Francine pushed her chair back, looked toward the door. She fit her feet into her white clogs. When she stood, Colville hurried to unlock the door, to hold it open. She touched his shoulder, stepped past him, outside.

He stood there watching as she drove away; then her car turned a corner and he couldn't see it anymore.

6

HAD HE SLEPT? It didn't matter. He felt rested enough, full of anticipation, setting out deeper into where he was going. His skin prickled; he turned a slow circle: houses below, mountains, bare trees. No faces that he could see, looking back.

He'd left the motel room at dawn, hiked across town, through neighborhoods and parking lots, beside highways. He'd stood on traffic islands as school buses rolled past, children's faces looking out.

He'd found himself inside an enormous sporting goods store with a complicated taxidermy display in its center—bears and bobcats, a mountain lion eating a rabbit, raccoons climbing a tree—where he bought the tiny tent and the subzero sleeping bag he carried now, attached to his frame pack. He bought hiking boots and gaiters, wool socks, snowshoes, freeze-dried ice cream and buffalo jerky.

Now he carried it all, along with everything else. Sweating, he paused to rest; he stepped off the road, past the half-built houses, up into the foothills where he had searched so many times. He checked Francine's house, far below, every few steps. Eventually, there was movement there—the black dog, let out into the back yard by Wells. Many mornings, Colville had watched as Francine herself came out. From here, he'd watched her car make its turn at the corner and slide away toward downtown, aiming at the hospital. This morning, her car was already gone.

Frost lined the shadows white, the ground wet where the sun

had reached. Colville zigzagged through the scrub, higher, then along a slight ridge, into some taller bushes. The ground slanted down unexpectedly; he slid along a gravelly slope into a hidden depression about ten feet square. A few old beer cans rested amid charred logs in a circle of blackened stones. A low cave had been cut into the slope; in its mouth rested a metal pipe with rough concrete around each end. Colville set down his pack and tried to lift the pipe — it looked like a barbell — but it was far too heavy. He couldn't move it at all.

Next he began unpacking. The three green books of the I AM activity, others by the Messenger herself: *Saint Germain's Prophecy for the New Millennium; Violet Flame to Heal Body, Mind and Soul; How to Work with Angels.* He took out the tape recorder — he felt the energy coiled in the cassette tapes, those dictations, the Messenger's voice still echoing, vibrating inside him — and wrapped it with everything else in heavy plastic garbage bags, two layers. Tying the bags tightly, he pushed them as deep into the cave as they would go.

A sound, above. Gravel slid down the slope, out from under the bushes. Slowly Colville straightened, turned, one arm up to hold back the glare and to protect himself. Then another noise, more gravel sliding; he saw the side of her face there, turning, the back of her head.

"Wait," he said. "Don't go. Talk to me."

She kept climbing until he could no longer see her, only the tall bushes still shaking as she went.

"You don't have to come down here," he said. "I'll come up, out in the open."

His pack lighter now, he scrambled back the way he'd come, sharp branches in his face, against his hands. He stumbled out onto the slope, his eyes already searching for her retreating figure, but the girl was just standing there, ten feet away. In jeans and tennis shoes, a blue sweatshirt. Her blue eyes were sharp and wary, her dark hair loose and tangled.

"What?" she said. "Don't stare at me."

"I wasn't."

"My sister's not dead, you know. If that's what you think."

"I know that," he said.

"I've seen you before." The girl looked up at the sky, then back down at him. "Out here. I've watched you."

"I believe it," he said.

"No one else is searching anymore," she said. "Do you know where she is?"

"What?" he said. "No, I don't."

"Are those snowshoes? What's your name?"

"Colville," he said. "Colville Young."

Neither of them moved. The wind ruffled the bushes behind him, a soft-edged sound. The sky turned lighter and the clouds slid across it, their edges barely visible against each other.

"Did your tooth fall out?" she said. "I can see your tongue."

"Kind of," he said. "Yes."

"Is a new tooth growing?"

"No," he said, feeling the gap with the tip of his tongue. "I don't think so."

"Your adult tooth fell out?"

"Yes," he said.

The girl paused for a moment, her blue eyes on him. She looked away, down toward the houses, then back.

"What were you doing down there?" she said.

"Nothing," he said.

"You were hiding something," she said. "I saw."

"I was leaving some things behind," he said. "Things I don't need anymore, that I don't want to carry anymore."

The girl looked doubtful, glaring past him at the bushes. "So why'd you carry it all the way up here if you don't need it?"

"I don't know," he said. "Maybe I'll need it some other time."

"Maybe it'll be gone, by then."

"Maybe," he said. "How old are you?"

"Seven."

"Does anyone know where you are?"

"No," she said. "I'm supposed to be at school." She glanced away, down the slope, as if expecting to see someone coming after her.

"What's your name?" he said.

"You were supposed to ask me that right after I asked you."

"I was?"

"Yes."

"Your sister," he said. "When I came here, a week ago, I was certain I would find her."

"And you didn't."

"I don't think she's dead," he said. "She's alive — she's just not here."

"Is she coming back?"

"I lost a brother," he said. "His name was Moses. But the thing of it is, I didn't really lose him. Not really, exactly. I carry him around with me, wherever I go."

"Is he dead?"

"Yes, in a way."

"You carry him?"

"Inside," he said.

"My name's Della." She kicked a pebble without watching it skitter away. "I have to go."

"All right," he said. "Nice to meet you, Della. I'm glad. I'm glad we agree about your sister."

"But you don't know—"

"No," he said. "But there's plenty of things I don't know that I'm trying to find out about."

"Bye," she said, turning away.

He expected the girl to head down the slope toward her house, but she went in the other direction, climbing along the ridge, not looking back. He didn't follow her; instead he turned and looked down over the city, the neighborhoods stretching up toward him.

It took a moment to locate the girl's house — usually he looked for the round black shape of the trampoline, but it was no longer there. Taken away. Now her house looked so much like the other houses on the block, it was hard to distinguish. Two houses over, Francine's driveway was empty now, the blue truck gone, the back yard surrounded by fence. And there, on top of the picnic table as if trying to see higher, to get his attention, stood the black dog.

Colville tightened the straps of his pack and began to descend in long switchbacks, careful not to trip or lose his balance. The wind sliced around him; it felt colder now than it had on the way up.

The dog did not bark as he approached. It saw him and wagged its tail, leapt down from the picnic table so he could no longer see it.

Now he was against the fence. He could hear the dog whining, see its wet snout pushing through the narrow gaps in the boards, its tongue trying to lick at his fingers.

"Yes," he said, whispering. "Good boy. You recognize me, don't you? Don't you, boy? You were calling me? Here I am. I understand."

He did not want to climb the fence, to draw attention. Setting down his pack, he took out a tent stake and carefully bent the bottom of one board, then another, the nails groaning a little as they pulled out. He peeked through the gap; the dog sat watching, waiting. As soon as the space was wide enough, he slithered through, then licked at Colville's hands, scratched at his boots, whined quietly.

Colville pushed the boards back flush, tapped at the nails. "Yes, yes," he said. "We're going now, we're going to do it."

He climbed again, the dog darting ahead and then returning, always checking where he was. Once they crossed the first slight rise, they were out of sight of the houses.

"Come!" he shouted, and the dog leapt back, leaned against his thigh as he unbuckled the leather collar. He read the metal tags, then threw the collar away into the scrub as hard as he could; the dog began to run after, to fetch it.

"Kilo! Leave it. Let it be."

Colville liked the feeling of it, not walking alone. He wondered, as he went the long way down, around the houses, whether the girl was somewhere on the ridge above, still watching him.

—

7

A DAY OF HITCHHIKING later, they were in the mountains, in Montana. Colville followed Kilo across a one-lane, wooden bridge. Ahead, new log mansions glowed on the hillside, against the steel-gray sky. Past them, above, the canyon opened and spread out. Colville had been up here once or twice, as a boy. Tom Miner Basin. He'd gone along with his father, who was wiring a house for another member of the Activity.

A brown Dodge rattled past, now, through the washboards, toward the bridge. An old man in a cowboy hat raised two fingers from his steering wheel rather than waving.

The second pickup — coming up from behind, ten minutes later — pulled over. The woman driving it rolled down her window.

"Going up the Basin," Colville said before she could ask. "Can my dog get in? He can ride in the back, if you'd rather."

"Bring him in," she said. "Shovel and jack sliding around back there might kill him."

Colville swung his pack alongside a bale of hay, then got into the cab after Kilo and slammed the door.

They were moving, climbing. Kilo licked at the woman's ear, and she laughed. She wore a bright orange down vest under a blue Walls jacket, a red silk scarf tight around her neck. Snowmobile boots. Her dark hair had strands of gray in it and was tucked under a black-and-red-checked cap, its earflaps down.

"So who you headed to see?" she said.

"What?"

"Whose place am I taking you to?"

"No one's," he said.

They passed four horses in a corral, then two llamas. The back of the truck fishtailed a little as they climbed a big switchback. Ahead, the basin spread out, mountains on either side.

"Have to put on the chains one day soon," she said.

"I'm heading up to the top," Colville said. "The campground, there."

They passed the fancy gate to a fly-fishing lodge, small ranches, barns, fields of snow with horses and cattle standing in them.

"It's smart to travel with a dog," she said. "I doubt I would've stopped if you were alone. You hunting?"

"No."

"I thought, what with your coat. Seen some bow hunters around."

Colville looked down at the fabric of his new parka — tan camouflage, twigs and moss and leaves — then out the window again. Dark clusters, herds of cattle or elk, mottled the benches and higher slopes.

"Are you crying?" she said.

"No," he said. "No, I'm not." He wiped at his eyes, looked away.

Higher, they passed stone houses, gates and fences. The buildings were less frequent as they climbed, as the road leveled, its surface now white with untracked snow.

"I've only been here in the summer," he said. "When I was a boy. I hiked with my dad to see some caves, a petrified forest."

"Where you from?"

"Here," he said. "I grew up in the church, and then we moved away."

"I got a few friends used to be in it." Slowing, the woman shifted the truck into four-wheel drive. "What a mess."

It seemed she wanted to say more, but she didn't; they rode in silence again until they reached the sign for the campground.

Carefully she turned the truck around, then shifted out of gear and looked over at him.

"You all right? It'll be dark soon."

"Not for a couple hours." He opened the door, the cold sharp in his face.

"Everything's closed down for the season. There's no one up there, nothing."

"I'm snow camping," he said.

"So why do you need a campground?"

"I don't," he said. "Come on, Kilo."

He closed the door and the pickup moved slowly and silently away across the whiteness, beneath the dull sky, its red taillights growing smaller. Kilo whined, sitting there at Colville's feet, black tail sweeping back and forth.

"All right, then. Here we are."

The snow underfoot was only an inch, two inches deep, but it drifted deeper, off the road. Setting down his pack, he took off his jacket, zipped in the down insert, then pulled on the insulated overalls. Camouflage, they matched his coat: tan, with twigs and leaves. It reminded him of the uniform Moses had shown him for Afghanistan, the desert camouflage that looked like it had been made inside a computer, digitized.

He did not put on his snowshoes. Not yet. He did not wipe away the tears as he walked past the scattered picnic tables, all the campsites frozen and long empty, thick chains on the door of the bathroom. He knocked on a brown metal bear box and it echoed, its door swinging open. It was too late for grizzlies; he hoped that was true. Were there wolves, now? He couldn't remember if they were back, how all that discussion had turned out.

He walked a quarter mile down the road, Kilo trotting alongside him, in the tire tracks of the woman's truck. The shadows and the snowdrifts made it difficult to see where the water snaked down, off to the side of the road; when Colville found it, he turned right, following the rise, along half-frozen Sheep Creek, up under the lodgepole and white pines, the spruce and Doug fir. Snow sifted down, a squirrel or raccoon or possum or only the wind in the branches above. He glanced upward. Nothing.

They passed around petrified stumps, jagged and snarled. The ground grew steeper, the snow deeper, the shadows darker. Buckling on his snowshoes, he took out his quilted brown balaclava, pulled it over his head, and kept moving, slapping his way up a long slope. Kilo snapped at the snowshoes, at first, then fell back.

Were birds following him, leaping and darting from branch to branch? Were elk drifting in a silent herd just on the other side of this line of trees, slipping back whenever Colville turned to look at them straight on? How many animals were around him right now? Elk, bears, wolves and coyotes; raccoons, rabbits, squirrels and mice. Traveling in herds and packs, hibernating in caves and underground. Birds slicing through the air — closer, farther away.

And then there were all the Elementals and Entities thick in the air, as invisible in daylight as in the darkness of night. Was he feeling them now, close around him? And how could he know? He'd never known how to be certain which was which. Elementals, the nature spirits, had to be here, invisible — yet so were the Entities, who were more likely to lead his thoughts astray. Entities were caught between, disembodied beings that hadn't balanced their Light and couldn't ascend to the higher planes, that wished to attach themselves to the magnet of his heart. He shivered, squinted up into the trees' dark branches; he thought of Forcefields, made up of mankind's wrong thought and feeling, some as small as a person's hand, others drifting like vast clouds, casting shadows that suddenly changed his emotions, his energy. Archangel Michael had a special branch of his legion that broke up these fields, into smaller pieces.

Under his breath, Colville rattled through an Archangel Michael, a Tube of Light. That helped. He followed Kilo as they crested the ridge, descended along a canyon to another creek. Taking out the map, he switched on the headlamp. Lion Creek, it had to be. He felt more confident with each step, a vibration that grew, that pulled him along with a certainty beyond any map. This was the back way, a route he had never taken—that no one had ever taken, as far as he knew. He had no choice. If he'd tried to go straight up the canyon, to the Heart—through Corwin Springs, past King Arthur's Court and the rest of the buildings—he'd have been seen by the members of the Activity, whoever they were now. They would question him, turn him away, or worse.

The headlamp's yellow circle slid along the snow in front of him, Kilo's hind legs and tail cutting into the beam. They climbed a gentle slope, silent now, the only sound their breathing. At the top of the ridge, Colville looked down and saw faint lights, the windows of ranch houses a mile away. Cinnabar Basin.

He stayed in the trees, backtracked out of sight of the valley and houses below. The temperature was falling, the cold on him quick; he jogged, slapping his mittens together, snapping branches from deadfalls, dragging wood together for a fire. At first Kilo followed, back and forth; then he settled down near the pack and simply watched as the wood was piled higher.

The ridge hid the flames of the fire from the houses below, and also hid the beam of his headlamp as he unpacked his sleeping bag, set up his tent. He scooped pine needles, softened the space beneath the tarp, then hooked the two curved poles into the tent—a bivy sack, really, a long tube big enough for just one person—and attached the fly, pegged it down, added more wood to the fire. Sparks crackled, shot upward toward the dark branches. Kilo sat close to the warmth of the flames.

"Hungry?" Colville poured some dog food into the bowl, then headed out of the trees with his collapsible bucket and scooped up some snow to melt for water. He returned to the glow of the fire, the dog happily eating, the camp all set up.

"So far, so good," he said. "We have to be happy about how it's gone so far."

He readied everything, eating half a sandwich from lunch as he walked in tight circles around the fire. One way, then the other, to warm his left side, his right. He pulled his arms inside the body of his jacket, where it was warmer. When he twisted at the waist, the jacket's arms swung loose and slapped his body; the sound was exactly the same as when he'd done this as a boy.

◆

Much later, he awakened to Kilo's claws scratching his rib cage. The dog wanted to get out, but Colville held him still, one hand over his snout. A strange whistling filled the darkness, a high-pitched and guttural call. The fire had burned down, out. Was it snowing? The moonlight shone faintly. Footsteps, silence, another call. And then, in silhouette, a long line of elk shuffled past, only twenty feet away. Colville could smell them, musty and sour; Kilo's body tensed, his hair rose up. The calls, so sudden and strange, caught right under the skin, floated back even after they were gone.

We started the school day with twenty minutes of decrees, trying to visualize what the words said, trying not to think of anything else. We were taught that there was a secret-ray chakra in the center of each of our hands. We held our hands cupped when we decreed, so these chakras would hold more Light. Even the babies learned to decree; they were held in teachers' laps while the teachers decreed and clapped the babies' hands.

We had regular classes, like reading, math, and geography, as well as the spiritual teachings. It was all Montessori, with plants everywhere and shelves of stones, felt animals and sandpaper letters and wooden blocks, art supplies. Our classroom was in the basement of someone's house, but we called it an academy, treated it like an important place. Maya's school was in someone's attic, a half mile away from our school. My mom was our fourth- and fifth-grade teacher, and Colville was in class with me.

Sometimes the books we studied had words or sentences or paragraphs blacked out with marker, things we weren't supposed to know, and sometimes in the picture books whole pages were torn out or missing. That made things hard to follow.

We had to avoid pictures of animals talking or doing anything like a person, since animals were incomplete expressions, still changing to be like us one day. If you looked at a talking fox, you might take on the qualities of being foxy or cunning or deceitful. That was the Teaching. When we watched a videotape of *Fantasia,* the hippos were dancing and we were all told to cross our arms across our hearts, and to cross our legs, so that we wouldn't absorb what we were watching. It's funny, we had a little television, and a VCR set atop a bookcase, and we all sat at our desks with our arms crossed, watching so carefully.

One time we were watching another videotape. The digital numbers counting up on the VCR were as interesting to me as the movie, and I also watched the two windows up behind the television, two more squares of light, right at the level of the ground. A piece of sagebrush blew past, someone's feet in heavy boots walked by, a black dog sniffed along.

I felt my mom standing behind me, the pull of her body as she watched with us. She treated me like a regular student, and I wasn't to call her Mom like I did at home.

This videotape was all about how geography was going to change in the next five years. Our Activity had left California and come to Montana because the Ascended Masters had said California was going to break off from the continent and sink into the ocean. California, Oregon, even Idaho might sink away like that. Montana was all right; we were on good tectonic plates. A man's voice told us this, and on the screen the colored map showed the continents crack and the shape of the edges change as those states sank away, all those people lost and drowned.

Then the door of the classroom opened. There was no knock, no warning. The television was silent, switched off right away. The whole room got brighter.

It was the Messenger. Standing in the doorway without moving at all and looking at us with her sharp eyes, without even blinking. She wore a pastel blue pantsuit and matching pumps, like she was going to a business meeting. Her dark hair puffed around her head, swooping down in back. The ten rings on her fingers glinted, shining on us. It was silent for at least a minute before she spoke.

She told us that we were her children, that she was our mother, that she was our father's mother and our mother's mother. She used her own voice, not the echoing voices of the Ascended Masters. She did not raise her voice and it was already inside your head, like it didn't travel through the air; it just appeared, a vibration in your mind. We listened. We hardly breathed.

The Messenger often spoke to thousands of adults at once; she traveled in the higher planes and communicated directly with the Masters. She had decided to stay behind on earth and she had decided to come and talk to us, in our classroom. We knew when we saw her that she was not like us, and also that we could be Messengers if we worked hard, in our words and actions and decrees.

Energy radiated from her, a vibration that wasn't hot or cold, just a shiver in your blood circling in you with more electricity, the power growing. My body ached like I wanted to come out of my skin, and I glanced at my mom, to see if something might be wrong. The Messenger almost never came to Glastonbury, and it was always a surprise like this; there was no time to clean or prepare. Sometimes in the past Mom had fainted when decreeing, had been taken from her body. She was sensitive that way. Just being in the same room as the Messenger could do it, overload her system.

The Messenger told us that her heart was great enough to burn up all the darknesses in our hearts. She said she'd been playing in a sandbox, when she was a girl, and the scene had shifted to another frequency and she had found herself playing in the sand along the Nile River in Egypt. The Messenger had lived as Nefertiti, and as Marie Antoinette, and Queen Guinevere. I felt her eyes travel across the skin of my face, a warm ray washing over me, sliding away. The Messenger then closed her eyes for a moment and turned her face farther away from me. I felt a dimness like a shade across a lamp, and then the light returned.

She pointed at me, then, and she pointed at Colville. She told us that our paths were all intertwined. The two of you, she said. All intertwined. You must help each other in every way you can.

8

FRANCINE DROVE SOUTH from Boise, through Mountain Home and Idaho Falls. At Pocatello, she angled north, past Rexburg and Ashton, St. Anthony. The jagged silhouettes of the Tetons rose on the right. She switched on the high beams and the darkness reflected back at her. She switched them all the way off for a moment, and the stars leapt up in the windshield, the sky blackening.

Since she'd spoken with Colville in the motel, hours ago, she'd been imagining that she was being observed: an aerial view of the car in the darkness, her face staring through the windshield as she passed the exits, the dim glow of West Yellowstone, her profile unmoving as she continued up the narrow canyons, past the ski slopes, through the Gallatin Gateway. Past signs for Henry's Lake, for Hebgen Lake. Bozeman was less than a hundred miles away.

A semitrailer rattled past, startling her. She had to stay awake, to be more careful. She slowed, accelerated, felt in her pocket for the wooden heart, carved so long ago, sanded smooth.

◆

There was a light on in the back of Maya's house. Francine pulled into the yard, parked behind the truck. The baby shifted inside her as she stood up, crossed the driveway. When she rang the doorbell, another light came on inside the house, and then the porch light. Maya's face peeked through the window. The door opened.

"Little sister!" Maya said, hugging her. "You're enormous!"

"Thanks."

"You were always the skinny one." Maya looked past her, at the car. "You're all alone?" She wore boots, jeans, a jacket from the print shop where she was a manager; a streak of gray ran through her bangs. "You look tired," she said.

"It's a long drive. I have to pee."

Francine went down the hallway, closed the bathroom door; sitting there, she could hear her sister talking to the cat, the rattle of cat food in a bowl. She pulled up her pants, washed her hands, splashed cold water on her face.

"Hungry?" Maya stood waiting in the kitchen, the black cat at her feet. "I just got home. Work's been crazy." She took a pizza box from the refrigerator, set a slice on a plate, put it in the microwave. "Sit down, now. Tell me."

"Tell you what?"

"What's going on. Why you're here. How long you're staying."

"I wanted to come back, just for a day or two."

"Where's Wells?"

"Fine," she said. "At home. How are you doing?"

"Same as ever."

Francine poured herself a glass of water, sat down at the table, the kitchen surrounding her with all its shades of green: the refrigerator and dishwasher dark like the countertops, the linoleum paler. Even the phone was green. She heard a ticking and looked behind her; the baseboard heaters were coming on, heating up.

"Are you trying to change the subject?" Maya said.

"I've been feeling, I don't know," Francine said. "Sentimental. And I was thinking—"

"You missed me."

"It's having the baby, I think, that makes me wonder. That's the thing."

"What's the thing?"

"You know. All about Mom and Dad, I guess. Just being a parent."

Maya set the plate in front of her. Francine took a bite of the pizza, burned her tongue, put it down again.

"So you could have the baby anytime?"

"Not really. I mean, I could and I guess it would be all right, it could breathe air and everything. It wouldn't be the best."

"How does it feel?"

"Weird."

"That's all?"

"It's hard to describe. A little scary."

The lights hummed above. The windows reflected black. The clock on the stove said 10:15. It felt much later.

"I was thinking," Francine said. "I was thinking it might help me to go back to Glastonbury, to the shelter."

"The shelter?" Maya said. "It's such a mess, just mold and spiders."

"Do you still have the keys?"

"You should be taking it easy, Francine."

"So help me. Tomorrow morning."

"Tomorrow's a workday. We're way behind schedule."

"I'll go alone, then."

Francine looked at the crust in her hand, the slice of pizza already gone, then back across the table. There was a new crease in Maya's forehead, between her eyes, and new wrinkles around her mouth. She had had a few gray hairs before; now they had gathered in this swath of her bangs. Or perhaps all of her hair was gray and she'd dyed the rest. No, that wasn't like her.

"You should call Wells. Tell him you made it."

"I'll call him, a little later. I'm just so tired. You think I could take a shower?"

"Towels are in the closet. You know where."

Maya reached out, touching her shoulder as Francine kept

walking without slowing, down the hallway. It still felt strange to be on her feet, not driving, not to have the windshield framing her view. Kicking off her clogs, she turned on the fan in the bathroom, set a towel on the back of the toilet where she'd be able to reach it. She was standing there, half undressed, when Maya knocked on the door.

"Can I come in?"

"Yeah." She wrapped the towel around herself as the door swung open.

Maya had taken off her boots and now wore sheepskin slippers. "Well," she said. "There you are."

"You need something?"

"I just wanted to look at you."

"What?"

"Your body, I mean. Can I see it?"

"Why?"

"I don't know. I'm curious. Doesn't that make sense? My little sister, all pregnant?"

"No," Francine said. "I mean, I don't know if it makes sense. Not right now. I'm so tired. It's just weird."

"I'll set up the bed in the living room, then. I'm going to call it a night."

"Good night. And thank you."

The door closed again, and Francine was alone, feeling as if she'd done something wrong, wondering if she should call Maya back or walk naked into the living room. She stayed. She turned on the water in the tub, ran her hand under it. It took a little while to run hot, and then she pulled the lever so the shower sprayed down.

Stepping in, she kicked over Maya's shampoo and conditioner. She picked up the oatmeal soap, sniffed it, then rubbed it across her belly, her skin stretched tight. She closed her eyes, let the hot water beat down on her shoulders. The travel, she felt it in her bones; the yellow lines of the highway still slipped away on the back of her eyelids. She tried to bend down, to wash her feet; she couldn't even see them, couldn't get close. Her body felt like a costume, an attachment. And then the baby moved inside. She felt it first, and then saw the skin ripple, a movement like a hand beneath a sheet.

◆

She lay awake in the silence, the darkness, then hurried back and forth to the bathroom, the air cold against her bare legs until she was back under the warm blankets again. She felt the slats of the frame through the thin futon, smelled ashes in the fireplace. She couldn't sleep, couldn't get comfortable, turning from side to side. The baby wouldn't let her sleep on her stomach; she imagined its body curled up on itself, inside her; she imagined its soul, waiting and watching all this time, from the day she first met Wells, outside the university bookstore in Salt Lake City; it had listened to their conversations, all the great silliness, watched the camping trips and seen them get their marriage license at city hall. It had watched the morning she told Wells of the pregnancy, all the excitement and the worry. The soul watched Wells now, down in Boise, where he was probably asleep, believing she'd be back from work in the morning. To call him might wake him, and it would only let him know that she was not where he thought she was. He'd find that out eventually, and by then she'd be able to explain.

She listened to Maya upstairs, humming to herself as she walked around her bedroom, finally quieting down. The cat's footsteps were lighter, quicker, going up and down the stairs. It crossed the open doorway like a shadow.

The fourth time she got up to pee, she did not return to the futon, the living room. Instead, she quietly climbed the stairs, her hand sliding up the railing, guiding her to the hallway, the bedroom door.

Maya stirred when Francine lifted the comforter and slid in beside her.

"You asleep?"

"Was."

"Do you mind?"

"No. It's like old times."

"Yes." Francine felt herself begin to relax. Her sister smelled faintly of cinnamon, as she always had, the cold soles of her feet reaching back.

"Except for your belly pressing against me," Maya said. "That's new."

They both laughed, their sudden voices loud in the dark room. The cat whined, leapt down from the bed.

"What is it you want to talk about?"

"Nothing." Francine pulled the blanket higher, felt her sister breathing, her spine pressing back, easing away, returning. "It's just that I wanted to come back and see some things, by myself."

Outside, a car passed. There was the sound of wind, or rain.

"I can do it," Maya said. "I'll do it."

"Do what?"

"Go to the shelter tomorrow. In the afternoon? I should work, the morning."

"I might go earlier," Francine said. "You could meet me."

"It'd be easier to drive down together."

Francine wrapped her arm around her sister. She hugged her tightly, then loosened her hold. They breathed together, in the silence, almost asleep.

"Do you remember," Francine said, "our calls to Saint Germain, before we fell asleep? So we could visit his retreat while we were dreaming, our bodies in the trailer and our souls slipping off to some higher plane?"

"It was a crystal cave," Maya said, "in the Tetons." She giggled, shifted her legs beneath the sheets, her voice a whisper: "Beloved angels of Light, in the name of my own Real Self, I ask that you take me in my soul consciousness to the universities of the Spirit to be tutored. I thank you and accept it done this hour in full power."

"Tell me something," Francine said. "Something about Mom and Dad."

"What about them?"

"Something I don't know."

"I don't know what you don't know." Maya turned over to face Francine; it was hard to see her expression. "One thing I remember is how Dad used to rub Mom's feet, at the end of the day. At the dinner table, sometimes. I can remember how that looked, her feet in his big hands, and how he'd make up songs and sing them to her."

"Really?"

"Yes," Maya said. "I like to think about that sometimes."

9

When francine awakened and went downstairs to the kitchen, Maya was already gone. She'd left the key to the shelter on the counter, next to the green telephone, on top of a note: *I'll check in around noon. Hope my little sister slept well.*

Francine hadn't slept so soundly in weeks. She opened a cupboard, took out a cup. The telephone book was on the next shelf up, and she pulled it out, set it on the table, opened it as she waited for the teakettle to boil. Steinman, Murray Steinman. There the address was. It didn't seem that it should be so easy.

Half an hour later she was back in her car, driving slowly through the neighborhoods toward the edge of town. Houses spread out; neatly trimmed yards turned to pastures and fields, picket fences became barbed wire. She read the numbers on the mailboxes, counting them down. When she reached the address, she shifted out of gear and kept the motor running.

The house was set back from the road, one story, with two wings that met at a right angle. She didn't want anything in particular, didn't plan to get out of the car or knock on the door. She just wanted to see it, to feel what she felt. To sit here and imagine the Messenger inside, just through the wall, with voices in her head and perhaps gazing out a window or taking a nap or looking through a picture book, photographs. It seemed impossible.

In one corner of the pasture next door, sheep gathered, pressed together for warmth. Two shaggy llamas stood against the fence, closer, steam jerking from their mouths as they chewed their cuds. The sky above hung pale and gray, the sun a paler disk cut into it.

Then the front door of the ranch house opened. A person in a red hat and brown coveralls, zipping up a heavy coat, stepped out and walked around the side of the house. This person turned once, looking back out to the road, toward Francine, and waved.

Opening the car door, she switched off the ignition. She stood up and squinted. The person waved once more, seeming to indicate that Francine should follow, and disappeared around the back of the house.

Francine stumbled. The ground was uneven, mud that had frozen. She still wore her white work clogs; her hands were cold, and she couldn't balance with them in her pockets. As she caught sight, drew closer again, it seemed that the figure ahead was an old man, walking away from her, toward two shaggy horses who lifted their heads and tossed their manes at his approach. Francine kept following, along the outside of the fence, some of the strands of wire taut and new, others rusted and slack.

When she looked up, the man had stopped walking and still looked away, at the horses. They lifted their heavy hooves and lurched along, closer.

"Hello?" Francine said. "Hello?"

The man turned, the red hat almost falling off, held down with one gloved hand. Gray hair stuck down around an expressionless face, gray skin. It was actually a woman, an old woman, now only fifteen feet away. She took a step closer, looking at Francine.

"It's you!" the woman suddenly said. "Oh, yes, it's you. I thought you'd finally come. I remember. I remember. You think I don't remember, but I do remember."

She did not gesture, her hands at her sides. Her voice was ragged and low, a monotone. Nothing like the Messenger's voice; her eyes were not full of Light; they were unfocused even as she said she remembered.

"It's been a long time," Francine said.

"You and your sister — I've seen her, she used to come by."

The horses had reached the Messenger now; their bristly lips nibbled at the shoulders of her coat.

"Ah." She turned, smiling. "My friends. These are my friends. Here are my friends." She repeated these sentences, patting the horses' necks, then took an apple from each of her pockets, held them out.

Once the apples were gone, the horses tossed their heads, leaned against each other, waited. The Messenger clapped her gloved hands and they wheeled, clomped across the pasture.

"Mother," Francine said, the fence still between them.

The Messenger didn't seem to hear. She was singing something to herself, softly, her head nodding a melody as she stomped on gopher holes. She circled slowly around, spiraling closer, farther away.

"I'm going back there today," Francine said. "I'm going to have my own baby."

The Messenger stopped circling, stopped singing. She stepped even closer, now only five feet away and looking right through Francine.

"I know that," she said. "Of course you are. Everyone wants me to name the babies, everyone. All the names of everyone and then where my jewels are, too."

"No," Francine said. "That's not what I want."

"I remember you," the Messenger said. "You think I don't remember you, but I do remember you."

"Did my sister really come here?"

"Yes. Many days she comes. And the boy — you and the boy, you used to go everywhere together. I haven't seen him in a long time. No."

"We spent a lot of time together back then," Francine said. "I just saw him — "

"Of course you did," the Messenger said. "He's your brother, after all. You would do that."

"Mother —"

"The little boy, the little son, of course I see him, every day I see him."

Just as Francine realized that the Messenger had mistaken her, that the old lady was actually talking about her own sons and daughters — not Maya, or Colville, or Francine, herself — a voice shouted. A man stood at the back of the house, an open door behind him.

"Mother! Come inside now!" He was tall, with a pointed beard and a thick mustache; he wore a kind of bathrobe, blue nylon boots. "Come now, Mother!" he shouted. "Hurry, now."

The Messenger was already walking toward him, unsteady, her face watching the ground in front of her. She did not look back.

Francine stood where she was as they disappeared into the house. She didn't see any faces in the windows. No one came back outside to ask who she was, to ask her to leave. Shivering, she walked back along the fence line, past the house and across the yard. Her car waited for her out on the street. It was still warm when she climbed inside.

She did not return to Maya's house. Instead, she drove down Main Street, through the old downtown. Past the rearing white horse that spun above the door of the Army Navy Store, past the new art galleries and coffee shops, out onto the interstate.

Snow flurries drifted down at the top of the pass; as Francine descended the other side, they disappeared, and the sky opened up. A surprising blue, a blue that she remembered. Darker than it seemed a sky should be.

That day in the classroom, after the Messenger told me and Colville that our paths were intertwined, that we had to help each other, she began to leave. She told us to remember our Archangel Michaels, especially in these times. She told us to have fun on the path, and that our duty was to prove Light. The door closed silently behind her. I don't think she even touched the doorknob and it moved.

It was silent. We glanced up at the windows, hoping to catch sight of the Messenger's feet. We did not. It was as if she didn't have to walk past the window, as if she'd floated away.

We didn't turn the videotape on again; we didn't watch the end, to see what would become of the world. We all tried to work on mathematics. Hardly a pencil scratched a number. Our minds wouldn't sit still. And then the signal went off. Right away we were all lined up, ready.

The sky was so clear and blue, bright outside. The wind had disappeared; it was hard to know which way to lean. All across the hillsides, people were moving. Lines of children from all the schools, cars and trucks piled with mattresses and everything. Cars sped by, down below on the highway, driven by people who didn't know what was coming, who hadn't been warned or hadn't believed. I looked up into the blue sky, wondering if you could see a missile coming, how fast it would be, whether something next to you might just explode and you wouldn't know that something was coming at all, if the sound would be delayed and so would the sight. Only if we survived could we explain what had happened; or maybe we could explain it, just not from the earth.

Mom led us along the route we'd practiced before, the hard dirt road of Glastonbury. Two kids from our class peeled away from the line, up a path toward Liberty Lighthouse, their shelter. A truck rattled past, a duffel bag falling off and left behind. We kept walking. We each had a buddy, to keep track of and to keep track of us. In a moment like that, rushing, worrying, any kind of Entity might lead you away.

My buddy was Colville, and he walked right in front of me, kicking his feet along, hardly lifting them. He had this way of wearing his jacket where it hung over his shoulders and the arms were empty, his own arms out in front, through the zipper. So he looked like some kind of octopus, or half-octopus. Both of us were thinking about what the Messenger had said, how we were all intertwined, but we didn't say a word.

We passed the Kehoe shelter, the Kletter shelter, white pipes hooking up from underground so the hidden people would be able to breathe. My mom was shouting not to lag behind. It was so hard to go fast, wearing a skirt, and we were always wearing skirts and dresses, loose so our curves wouldn't show or so it wouldn't show if we were developing. I wasn't. Maya was, and I could see her ahead, coming down a slanted path to join us. She walked with her friend Courtney Stiller, laughing, and Courtney was wearing jeans, which we weren't supposed to wear. All the lines of our shelter, Lifesavers, were coming together near the opening, where the earth had been heaped up to cover everything.

We didn't slow as we passed my family's trailer; we went farther, down toward the mounds of fresh dirt. We passed a dump truck, a bulldozer. We climbed up to the top and looked down, fifty feet underground, to where the men were working.

In school I'd built a diorama of the workers on the Egyptian pyramids, and this was the same. If I held up my hand, it blocked a man out. That's how far down they were. The shelter then was open; the concrete was about to be poured, and then all the dirt would be pushed back over it. This day the bent redwood ribs showed like arches, and the rebar over them, the whole thing circular, like a huge doughnut that seventy people would live inside. I don't think I've ever been so proud of anything.

Through the ribs I could see the men, so busy, racing along. My dad was in charge, building all day every day, deciding what people should be doing. Then I saw him, waving up at me, shouting. His arms and face were all black with dirt except around his eyes, where he'd been wearing welding goggles. That's when I knew it was only another drill, that it was not the day, even though the Messenger had visited us. My father was smiling, down there, laughing like it was all the same to him whether the world ended or didn't end. He knew that everything was temporary.

10

WELLS AWAKENED ON the couch, white pages strewn around him. A few still rested on his chest; he held one out now, squinting: Francine, trying to sleep so far underground, surrounded by her family and yet separated from her friend by miles of dirt and stone.

When he sat up, pages slid to the floor. Kilo, sleeping there, lifted his head with a startled sound.

The dog followed Wells out of the living room, down the hallway. The door to the baby's room was open, the room empty, as was their bedroom. The bed still made, the blankets pulled tight. Wells picked up Francine's phone from her dresser, turned, and headed toward the kitchen.

It was almost ten o'clock; she should be home by now. He dialed the hospital, waited to be connected to her department. The woman who answered was not someone he knew.

"Francine's not working now. She's not here."

"When did she finish?"

"Pardon me?"

"She worked last night," he said.

"I don't think so. I believe she's gone on maternity leave. I can check the paperwork if you like."

"That's all right," he said, hanging up the phone. He knew that the woman was mistaken; if Francine wasn't at the hospital, she had to be here soon, on her way home.

Kilo was scratching to be let out. Wells took hold of his collar and opened the door; barefoot, he led the dog down the steps to the driveway, unlatched the wooden gate to the back yard, and let him loose.

The morning was cold. The air smelled like snow. Wells glanced up along the slope and for a moment thought he saw two figures — one taller, one shorter — standing on the distant ridge. Then they were gone and he couldn't find them again. Turning, he went back up the steps into the kitchen.

He started the coffeepot, got dressed. Five minutes passed, ten. Francine should have been home by now, and he didn't like waiting, and anything could have happened to her, somewhere between the hospital and home without her phone to call him with. He snatched his keys from their hook, headed outside, and climbed into his truck.

Down the street, around the corner, he accelerated to make it through a yellow light. This was the way she drove home; he thought it was. He passed under a billboard, the lost girl's huge, pale face staring and smiling down at him, and then a thought came to him, a suspicion. He turned suddenly, away from the path to the hospital. It would take only a moment to check, to be certain.

He pulled into the parking lot of the Econo Lodge, skidded to a stop. There was no one around. Hurrying to the door of room 12, he knocked twice, hard, then waited.

"Colville!" He slapped at the door with the flat of his hand; he pressed his ear close to the brass numbers. There was no sound inside. Nothing.

And then, farther down, he saw movement, a door opening. A man came out of the office. Bald, wearing a Boise State parka, a cigarette in one hand.

"He checked out this morning!" the man shouted, then coughed. "Room's empty!"

Wells began to step toward the man, to ask him if he knew

anything more, but just then the phone in his pocket began to ring. He pulled it out—it was Francine's phone, not his. When he flipped it open, he saw that it was Maya calling.

"Hello?" he said.

"I must have the wrong number—"

"Maya," he said. "It's Wells."

"Oh," she said. "Hi. I was supposed to call Francine, so I could meet her. You have her phone? I mean, obviously you do."

"Is she all right?" he said. "She's there?"

"I thought she called you."

"Is she all right?"

"She's fine," Maya said. "She's okay. Just visiting for a day."

"Is she alone?"

"What? Yes."

"Where are you meeting her?"

The reception crackled and snarled. Across the parking lot, the motel manager stood next to Wells's truck—its door was still open, and he'd forgotten to shut off the ignition. Steam twisted from its tailpipe.

"She's coming back to Boise tomorrow," Maya said. "I think that's her plan."

"So I'm just supposed to wait?"

"Everything's fine," Maya said. "Really, it's okay. I'll have her call you."

Wells closed the phone and put it back in his pocket. He drove home more slowly, retracing his path. When he reached the house, he parked in the driveway and sat there for a moment before climbing out.

"Kilo?" he said. "Here, boy."

But when he opened the gate, the dog did not come leaping out, as he usually did. Wells stepped into the back yard, scanned its perimeter. Empty. He looked up along the slope that led to the ridges, but there was no sign of the dog. Sometimes this happened; when neither Wells nor Francine was home, Kilo would find a way out of the yard, go searching for them. He always came back.

Inside, there was only the smell of burned coffee, last night's dishes in the sink. Wells walked into the living room. The pages were scattered white across the couch, spilled onto the floor. What would Francine say, if she came home to this? He'd like to hear it, for her to see these pages everywhere and to know that he'd read them all.

The fires came in 1988. They burned all through Yellowstone Park and came over the ridge, threatened the Heart. That's where we gathered, raising our voices: *Reverse the tides, Roll them back, Set all free*. The sky was all smoke, the mountains invisible, trees coming and going. I stood next to my mother, watching her face, the heat on my skin. The peanut butter and egg salad sandwiches we'd brought all tasted like smoke.

I chased after Colville when he called my name, broke away from where we all stood. We ran out along the edge of the deep pit being dug for the shelter, past the yellow bulldozers, through the tall, dry grass. We left beaten-down paths behind us.

Between the fire and all the people, animals gathered, herded down the slope by the flames. Elk and moose, raccoons and snakes and mice, all too worried to chase or fight, too afraid to eat each other.

Fires are energy made visible. When the flames came closer, descending the canyons, we wore wet bandannas over our faces. We prayed so hard. The heat bent the air, the heat in my throat. Voices rose up: *Reverse the tides, Roll them back, Set all free*. The voices rose up and the flames skirted the Heart. They didn't burn one tree.

11

COLVILLE AND KILO broke camp and started hiking before day-break. In the new snow they were able to follow the elks' path, which came upon and followed the Shooting Star trail south before tapering off. Up and over two ridges, in and out of stands of pine and aspen, along frozen creeks; they passed through charred deadfalls and sections where the ground was still black, new trees growing up through the remains of the fires.

And now they stood here, on the last ridge, overlooking the Heart. Below, the long rectangular indentations of the shelter showed clearly in the snow, the berms like drifts around them. The wide meadow was white, untracked. Had he expected the tents? The people? The energy spun up along the ridges; he felt it thick in his chest, a vibration that almost lifted him off the ground.

The soft snow eased his descent. He tried to slide a little in the snowshoes, to obscure his tracks, make them look less like what they were. Carefully he emerged from the last stand of trees, then circled the shelter, keeping a distance. Here in the icy snow, uncovered by wind, were vehicle tracks, chains on the tires. The watchman or maintenance man, most likely, checking in, sometime in the recent past.

Someone would come, would unlock the door, and Colville would have to wait, prepare himself, figure out how to get inside when that happened. Meanwhile, he'd trust that he had enough food to last until he could get to the provisions inside.

"Stay close, Kilo."

Colville didn't approach the large metal door; he could see the locks all over it from where he stood, fifty feet away. Instead he walked the perimeter of the shelter, up along the berm. Two low turrets rose above the surface, ten-foot antennas like whips above them. Thin rectangular windows, the only way to see out when one was inside, glinted beneath the snow above them.

Walking slowly, carefully, he uncovered one round escape hatch, then the next. Two feet across, round and made of concrete, each hatch was an inset circle with a hairline gap around it, impossible to pry open. He kept on, around the perimeter, the cold wind blowing snow in every direction.

As he approached the third hatch, at the shelter's corner, he could see that the snow had already been brushed away from it. Closer, he realized that the lid was not closed, that something – a slim metal rasp – was wedged in the gap. He took his hand from its mitten, fit his fingertips inside, and lifted the cover on its hinge, open.

A damp smell rose from the darkness. The concrete cylinder stretched down, steel rungs along its inside. Colville leaned close, listening, the warmer air rushing past him, up from below. He lowered his pack into the opening, past the counterweight and the latch, then dropped it, listening as it rattled away, as it echoed with a solid *whump* when it hit bottom. Next he called Kilo, picked the dog up in one arm; he swung one leg inside the cylinder, then the other. One-handed, he descended, slipping into the darkness.

They emerged at the bottom into a rounded hallway. Only a few emergency lights shone, pale in the ceiling. Colville knew exactly where he was.

"Easy," he whispered. He stepped carefully from the ladder, unable to see his feet, almost tripping over his pack as he shuffled down the hallway, past the doors of other families' quarters. He stopped at his own, pushed it open.

Taking the headlamp from his pocket, he clicked it on, off: the bunks, the faded purple seat belts across them, the bookcases, the shelves of clothes. Illuminated for an instant, gone, glowing on his retinas.

The room itself was a corrugated pipe on its side, round; there was storage underneath the bottom bed. Kneeling in the darkness, he slid the flooring aside, kicked whatever was stored there to one end, took off his hat, his jacket, and dropped them inside. It had been days since he had been so warm — this far underground the atmosphere was like a cave's, the temperature somewhere near sixty degrees. Heat came from the geothermal energy below as well, or at least people had always said so.

He swiveled around to sit on the mattress. First he took two protein bars from his pack; then he drank from the insulated container, poured some water into the bowl-like top for Kilo. The only sound beyond the dog's drinking was the distant rush of wind; he remembered his mother saying it would be like living inside a seashell, his father answering that they'd no longer hear it, after a week or so, especially with the noise of all the other people living so close.

Sitting like this on the bunk, Colville could hardly believe he was inside; then again, he felt like he was home, that he could be nowhere else. He tightened the strap around his head, switched his headlamp back on. Its round beam slid along the floor, across the black shape of the dog, up onto the wall.

A wide sheet of white paper hung from rusted tacks: his father's diagram of the shelter. Colville started his rough copy not with the outer walls, but by drawing an X where he stood and then drawing the walls right around him, the section of shelter where he stood. This section, one of six, was for families — different numbers of bunks, single and double, every conceivable space used for storage, nothing wasted. The pod where he stood would have held one hundred and twenty people; with the other five, around seven hundred, total, and in the Deep Core Storage enough food for seven years for everyone.

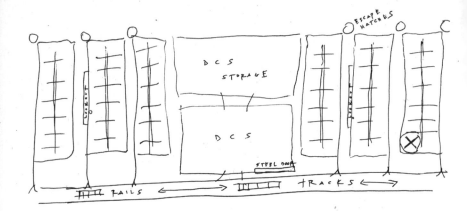

As he sketched the lines, Colville thought of all the work, the hugeness of it all. His father had spoken of the long sections of the shelter barely fitting through the narrow canyon, being brought up on trucks, piece by piece. He remembered men reading army surplus catalogs in the lunchroom; piles of packages arrived from Eddie Bauer and L.L. Bean; big wooden boxes were delivered on trucks, all the equipment that was still here, underground, around him now. His father had wired the whole shelter, and his mother had worked so hard — she'd helped gather and organize, dehydrated and packaged the food, even when the Messenger said she should rest.

Colville carefully folded the paper when his sketch was done and put it in his pocket. He was hot, nearly sweating; he peeled off his coveralls, dropped them into the hollow space beneath the bunks. Next he slid his frame pack in and fit the piece of plywood back over it all.

His headlamp's beam shone out the doorway into the hall, onto his family's storage shelves there, all his father's books. He stepped closer. *How to Stay Alive in the Woods; How to Live with Low-Level Radiation: A Nutritional Guide;* Sun Tzu's *Art of War;* the Boy Scouts' *Fieldbook; Life After Doomsday; Project: Readiness.* He reached out, but he didn't touch them. *Where There Is No*

Dentist; The Tracker; Tom Brown's Guide to Wilderness Survival;
The Twelfth Planet; Out-of-Place Artifacts: What Early Visitors
Left Behind.

"Okay," he said, scratching Kilo's head. "Time to look around."

The doors to the tunnel, he'd always loved them; they looked like the doors on a submarine: rounded, with a bar that locked down from either side, a black rubber gasket around the edge that was now dry and cracked. He bent down to get through, kicked the metal rails on the tunnel's floor.

The carts were heavy, probably for mining, and could hold a lot, could be pushed in long lines as they had been before that night in 1990, piled high with sleeping bags and books and people's personal belongings, everything they'd need. He'd ridden the carts as a boy, flat on his back and kicking the corrugated top of the tunnel to scoot himself along the whole length of the shelter.

"Here, Kilo," he said, and hoisted the dog up, kept him from leaping off. The cart's metal wheels squeaked as they passed the door to another pod — one for unmarried people, if he remembered correctly — and kept on deeper into the darkness.

At the next door he stopped pushing the cart and lifted Kilo out, then followed him into a small antechamber. Dim fluorescent lights hummed, flickered above. A table with a plywood top, hammers on it; an electric drill; a chain saw with the chain loose, tangled on itself. On the wall, a clipboard hung from a nail. Colville didn't touch it; he just leaned close. Names, dates, times, check marks. Mostly it was James, sometimes it was Stephen. Someone always came on Tuesday, usually in the afternoon. Today was Thursday, or it was Friday; he would have to keep better track.

Kilo sniffed over to the steel door, whined, returned. He could smell the world outside.

"Come on, boy."

Deeper, past the tool room — its walls of picks and shovels, hammers, bolt cutters, pliers and wrenches — and around the generators and the stationary bicycles. Now Colville stood in the DCS, the first of its two chambers. No one ever called it the Deep Core Storage, really; the initials were enough. A few dim safety lights glowed in the ceiling, fifty feet above, and pallets of stores were stacked almost all the way to the very top. The beam of his headlamp reflected off the clear plastic shrink wrap, lit the tags. *Dried Fruit, Rice, Seaweed, Flour.* He walked down the aisle between the towers. His footsteps echoed; he'd heard there was a secret hollow space beneath this floor, filled with thousands of coins, gold and silver, machine guns and ammunition.

Suddenly, a loud snap, off to his left, a high-pitched cry, and then Kilo came shooting down an aisle into Colville's legs.

"Mousetraps. I said to stay close."

They went deeper, through the gap where the chamber narrowed and opened up into the second vast space. Here the mildew was stronger; the air was thicker; the vibrations clustered, almost hummed. His headlamp shone into darkness, lit only suspended dust. Objects arose as if surfacing from deep and murky water: carts of folding chairs stacked ten feet high, the shadowy shapes of the backup generators in the electrical room, then the boxes and boxes with dates written in black marker: 11/20/82, 4/6/84, 7/4/85.

At the far end of the chamber, the round beam of his lamp circled a light switch. He knew it was a risk — no doubt someone watched the electric bills, the kilowatt hours, and any change would draw attention — but for one instant he switched it on, to see it all at once and not in pieces. The image flashed in his mind even after he switched the light off: here was the meeting room; the large plastic pieces of the altar; boxes stacked high, surrounded by mousetraps, a few with the dried corpses of mice in them. The smell all around him was mice, mixed with old paper. The boxes were full of dictations, and the danger was that the mice would eat all the important words, the warnings and promises of the Ascended Masters that had passed through the Messenger into the air, before being set down on paper.

The darkness closed down again, all the time collapsing, the air heavy around him. Was it nighttime? He needed to rest, to sleep. Carefully, he led Kilo back through the DCS, into the tunnel, and returned to the pod that housed his family's quarters.

Once there, he uncovered the storage space in the floor and sorted through his things. He left the sleeping bag behind, stuffed everything else into his pack, then lifted another section of the floor. The space here was full of shoes; he pushed them all to one end, then laid his pack down, slid the cover over.

There was enough room in the floor for both of them — more than in the tent last night, and it was also warmer. Colville lay flat, the dog curled in the space between his legs. He slid the plywood over the top of them, leaving the narrowest gap to breathe through.

In that darkness he could almost hear the decrees echoing up and down the passageways; he could almost see his mother, so pregnant, decreeing with the other women, all cutting the air with their two-foot swords — rending the bad energy, slicing it loose from the air around them. His father had been coming and going, wire cutters in one hand, a voltmeter in the other. Colville had just sat on the top bunk that night, watching and listening, buckling and unbuckling the seat belt that was there in case of earthquakes or a close missile strike.

He lay still. The way he felt, it was as if right now were twenty years ago. Decrees ran through his mind, memories of being in the top bunk, his parents beneath him, waiting in the darkness, right here in this room.

And then, now, he heard a different sound. Not only the shelter's quiet roar; a howling, higher-pitched. His forehead butted the plywood as he tensed, tried to hear, to figure it. Finally he slid the cover away. He carried his boots and his headlamp as he crept past the books on their shelves, down the hallway, toward the hatch.

The sound rose higher as he approached. Not voices, not foot-steps. It gusted, it almost whistled. He'd left the hatch open; the wind had picked up and now howled across the opening, like a person blowing across the mouth of a bottle.

In his stocking feet, he climbed the metal rungs, up the narrow cylinder. The air turned colder as he ascended. He stuck his head out, above the surface, and his skin stung, the hairs in his nostrils brittle. Squinting across the glowing white expanse, he could see no movement, no one approaching, no person or animal.

He stood half in the hatch, his head and torso exposed to the bitter cold. The energy hummed around him, the landscape all alive. He laughed aloud, took a deep breath. Heavy snowflakes drifted down out of the dark sky. No stars, no moon. The snow already filled his footprints from earlier today, and Kilo's paw prints. Colville looked behind him, to each side. Descending, he took hold of the rope just above the counterweight and lifted. The hatch slapped shut gently above his head. The wind's howling was gone at once, and silence thickened around him.

12

THERE WERE EIGHT carts, all together, and Colville pushed
seven of them to one end of the tunnel, out of the way. He found
an oil can in the tool room and lubricated the metal wheels of the
eighth cart until it ran smoothly, with a low metallic hiss. Lying
on his back, holding Kilo pressed against him, he kicked along
the ceiling of the tunnel and the cart shot through the darkness.
He covered the hundred yards in less than thirty seconds. To slow
down, he let the toes of his boots drag along the corrugated metal
above.

He wandered, he searched. His headlamp's beam shone like
a bright rope that pulled him deeper into the darkness, toward
new discoveries. Turning corners, he still expected to meet the
boys he'd known, or their parents, to hear decrees or see the men
with the radiation gauges, measuring everyone who came in from
outside. He wore a pair of his father's tennis shoes, their laces
replaced with wire. The down vest, too — he could remember his
father wearing it; when he pulled it out of the cubby, the black
electrical tape that had been used to patch it fell off, slippery now
on both sides. As he walked, he nervously held one hand over the
rip, as if the little white feathers might alert someone to his presence.

One family's stash of Jane Austen novels, cans of chewing to-
bacco hidden inside a wall, swords used for some of the blasting
and rending decrees. He found axes and knives, hidden behind
beams in ceilings, and dolls with dusty hair, chewed hands and

feet. Folded-up body bags, stored next to white radiation suits. A record player, albums of Christmas music. All of the six dormitory pods were more or less the same, only laid out slightly differently. There were the rooms where people slept, then the toilets and showers — all the water turned off, now — a decontamination chamber, a kitchen, and a common area where decree sessions and school could be held.

He stood in one such common area and shone his headlamp along the alphabet running letter by letter along the top of the wall, where it met the ceiling. He sat in the tiny desk where he might have studied, for months or years, if things had gone a different way.

The desk was the same as the ones they'd had in Glastonbury, back in the classroom with Francine. Francine's mother was their teacher. She had been patient with him; she had taught them so many decrees. She decreed along with them, and even in the classroom the Light would suddenly come into her, sometimes, and knock her down, knock her out as if she'd suddenly fallen asleep. It would take her a while to return to this plane. She had been meditating and decreeing when she died, too. She was overcome; her heart just came apart, filled with Light. Some said she'd ascended right there and then.

Kilo would not sit still, would not stop circling between the desks with his head up, his back arched. Suddenly he barked at the wall. Once, twice, the sound echoing.

"Here." Colville's voice was a hiss. He bent down, his hand around the dog's snout. The air settled; there was no sound.

Only the air didn't quite settle, despite its silence. It felt different. Heavier, the energy pulsing in jagged waves around the dark room. He shone his light along the wall, stepped closer, pulled furniture away. Shadows, spider webs, the word TRANSMUTA-TION in black marker. He paused at an altar, hesitant to touch, to disturb it. The light of his headlamp reflected off the glass in the frames that held the Masters, gazing out at him. Saint Germain, El Morya, Jesus Christ. Carefully he lifted the purple fabric that was draped over the table, then dropped onto his stomach.

Here was a door in the wall, behind and underneath the altar. A square door, perhaps two feet across. A silver lock hung from a metal hasp, the hasp's metal plate folding back over the screws, so they could not be pried loose or easily undone. Colville just stared, Kilo whining behind him. Heat came from the wall, too much energy seeping out. Had the lock trembled, vibrated, or was that the trembling of his head, the beam of his lamp? He didn't know whether the energy was good or bad, only that it was too much. Dragging himself backward, he felt the hem of the fabric lap over the top of his head like a huge hand, slipping away.

◆

Two big Isuzu generators stood bolted to the floor in one corner of the DCS; one was in case the line from Montana Power went out during or after the attack, the other in case the first generator failed. Their fuel rested in tanks buried near the shelter, filled with enough oil to last a long time, depending on everyone's usage of electricity.

If the second generator failed or the fuel ran out, there were these bicycles — also bolted to the floor, and attached to a large wheel that could turn out enough horsepower for the shelter's emergency needs. Colville's father had set this up, and now Colville rode the bikes. For exercise, not electricity — and mostly he rode in darkness, decreeing while keeping his ears alert, watching for Kilo's reactions.

As he rode, he glanced at the shadowy towers of stacked pallets in the DCS. Twenty feet away was the hiding place he'd made — a flap of plastic that looked solid, labeled as dried beans, but that was hollow inside. If he was surprised here, or cut off from the tunnel, he and the dog could be hidden in five seconds. He practiced leaping down from the bike, scooping up Kilo. It was as if they had never been here.

He ate a dried rice cake, a handful of tiny, silver dried fish, then the round chips of bananas that tasted like dust. Switching on his headlamp, he read about survival techniques, about the Messenger's visits to Atlantis in her earlier embodiments, about the Soviet cosmonauts who reported, in 1985, that they had seen seven large angels, floating in the atmosphere.

He pumped harder, his circling feet slipping a little on the pedals, his knees kicking up and down. A kind of charge built up in him, energy beyond simple heat. Closing his eyes, he imagined himself riding down a street, outside somewhere. The gravel roads of Glastonbury, under the sun, or the smooth city streets he'd known later. He could feel the sun, the wind, the sweetness of the air almost, and then he opened his eyes and there were the dark shapes of the generators again, hulking in the dim light. He couldn't look at them, or even at the silent, staring faces of the outlets on every wall, without thinking of his father threading the wires, tightening the connections. His father had always explained the energy of the Ascended Masters in electrical terms — how theirs was a kind of higher ether electricity that worked its way through suns and solar systems and then planets and bodies, the vibrations more and more condensed. A regular person couldn't withstand that energy, yet the Messenger had been able to take and listen to it, to step it down as a transformer would, to pass it through herself in the form of dictations, to pass it on to everyone.

Colville thought of his father and his mother — reminded by sleeping in the space they had prepared, where he could have spent seven years so close to them — yet his thoughts turned even more frequently to Moses. He knew that all this energy wound up and vibrating inside him, this Light, had once been inside his brother.

Still pedaling, Colville unzipped the pocket of his vest. First he pulled out the wrong piece of paper — the article from the *Spokane Spokesman-Review*, the lost girl's picture, her face, a fold cutting across the part in her hair — before he found what he was looking for, the last letter that Moses had written to him.

```
Colville,
    What up? I miss you. Everyone could use a big
brother out here. It's something else, the wait-
ing and waiting until your hoping for something
to happen and then someones shooting at you or
you see a dog blown up by an IED right in front
of you and you start hoping for these days like
now. Boring. Sand fleas. Bad music played too
loud. I'm taking care, and I'm good at this,
don't worry, and I'll write more later I just
wanted to say I'm thinking of you brother.
Moses
```

Moses was supposed to be born here in the shelter. What had been the plan for where he was going to sleep? And how would it have been — how strange to be born here, to be underground for so long and to know the world outside only through pictures in books? And then finally to go outside, where it would look nothing like the books, where everything would be burned up, blackened, covered in ash, and if there were animals they wouldn't be like those in the books? Or maybe there would be radioactive animals, all kinds of mutations, so many unknown living things.

13

THE DAY WAS BRIGHT and cold, the snow frozen into a hard crust that he could walk across without leaving any sign. Colville wore a white radiation suit, to be invisible against the snow. He lugged the white bucket, his toilet, up toward the trees to dump it.

Kilo ran ahead, delighted to be outside, zigzagging up the slope, disappearing into the trees. Colville looked back once, checking the hatch, always nervous that the door would somehow close. Turning, looking across the Heart, he squinted his eyes and imagined the snow gone, melted; he could almost see the white tents, could feel how it felt, chasing Francine through the tall grass with the smell of food cooking and the sound of the decrees humming everywhere, everything giving way to the Messenger's amplified voice, dictating the words of the Masters so forcefully that they echoed everywhere, seemed to emanate from the mountains.

Colville was almost to the trees when the air began to tremble. The vibrations came in waves; after a moment the sound itself rose, louder, all around him.

He dropped to the snow, crawled. Once he reached the trees, he squinted down across the white expanse. At first what he saw seemed like blowing snow, caught by a gust, and then perhaps a small animal, a dark round spot amid the whiteness. It came up from the road that led to the canyon, growing larger as it approached.

And then another black shape — Kilo, darting across the space between, circling toward the hatch, up across the slope, searching for him.

The sound grew, rattling the trees, as the shape approached. Sliding across the surface of the white snow, it was a creature half man and half machine, black and whining. An Entity. So fast, with so little friction. The light bent and shivered; all edges blurred. Colville looked away — at Kilo, still out in the open — then back to where the black shape rushed closer, throwing snow in all directions.

It slid to a stop, suddenly went silent. And a man, in a black jacket, with a balaclava over his face, leapt free and began to run. Toward the steel door, around the berm, suddenly out of sight.

Just as Colville began to understand, he heard another sound, something else approaching. A pickup truck came lurching through the powder, then stopped next to the snowmobile. Another man climbed out — heavier, in a green coat with a fur-lined collar — and followed the first one, beyond where Colville could see, toward the metal door. These men had to be the caretakers from the Activity, the names on the clipboard. James and Stephen. They were inside now, writing their names on the clipboard, switching on lights, walking through the passageways. Was today Tuesday? Had he left anything out that would draw their suspicion?

Now Kilo saw Colville, barked once, and raced into the trees.

"Quiet, boy. Here."

Wind rushed all through the Heart, ice crystals in the air, a whistling in the needles of the pines. The trees' shadows grew longer, disappeared as the sun went behind a cloud. Holding the dog tight, Colville wondered if they could make it to the hatch, if they should try.

A half-hour passed, perhaps an hour. The men returned. They didn't look around themselves, or up the slope to where Colville and Kilo were hidden. They didn't even glance toward the hatch that was propped open with the metal rasp; its lid was lifted only slightly in any case, and looked about the same as the others.

One of the men climbed onto the snowmobile, the other into the pickup. The snowmobile fishtailed, spraying white snow, and the truck carefully turned around, followed at a distance. They both disappeared down the canyon.

◆

When he wasn't exploring, decreeing, or exercising, Colville was reading. Survival manuals, dictations and decrees he'd never heard, new Teachings, piles of newspaper clippings. As he took food only from pallets up high, from their dark sides, he took only a few papers at a time and then returned them.

The Messenger warned about the Soviets and the Asians and Osama bin Laden; she wrote: *The West will be confronted by Asia in economic matters and by Islam in matters of religion.* She warned about technology: *Scientists have genetically engineered pigs and cows to bear human genes. They have grown a human ear on the back of a mouse. There was a time in Atlantis, too, when many people abandoned their first love and their allegiance to the divine Light within. Their scientists even went so far as to create grotesque forms of interbreeding man and animals through genetic engineering. These half-man, half-goat forms we read about in mythology are a soul memory of these events.*

Colville's eyes adjusted to the dimness — he'd brought so many batteries for the headlamp, but they would not last forever. Of the pale lights in the hallways, every third or fourth one still glowed. He gathered chairs from the many rooms and stacked them on each other as steadily as possible. Sitting that way — up close to the ceiling, wrapped in his sleeping bag, wearing a wool cap — he held his head to one side so light could shine on the words. He read the words, sometimes aloud; let the vibrations all pass through him, settle in the darkness around him. He paused only when he began to feel sleepy or cold, and then he climbed down to do calisthenics or practice yoga. Kilo, atop a padded camping mat, raised his head to watch.

The yellowed newspapers were all from the time of the shelter cycle. Articles about the Activity — anger in the surrounding community, geothermal disputes, herds of elk, buffalo escaping from Yellowstone Park — were surrounded by stories about President Bush's deficit plan, Gorbachev's glasnost. The mayor of Washington, D.C., admitted his drug use; the wall came down in Germany; an earthquake struck San Francisco.

He read some of the books that had fascinated him when he was a boy, which still entertained him yet now felt almost beside the point. Theories telling how civilization had evolved on earth twice, how the visitation of ancient astronauts was the return of descendants of ancient humans who had been separated from earthbound humans; how there were Egyptian artifacts that looked like tiny Space Shuttles, cave paintings in Italy where people seemed to wear space helmets, the famous Lid of Palenque whose carving showed the Mayan king inside a rocket ship.

The books he liked best were from his father's shelves: all the survivalist literature, the books about the classification of plants and animals. Sometimes there was scribbling in the margins; more often there were underlined passages, signaling what was important to his father, what he had gleaned: *Just as cold is actually the lack of heat, and as what we know as darkness is no more than the absence of light, so is getting lost an entirely negative state of affairs. We become lost not because of anything we do, but because of what we leave undone.* Colville unzipped his sleeping bag, climbed down, slid one book back and pulled out another. *We learned not only to camouflage our bodies, but also to camouflage our minds and spirits, moving into the place of invisibility. We became so adept at camouflage that neither animal nor man could detect us even if they looked directly at us.*

Often, reading, he would hear something — a creak in a wall or

the ceiling overhead, a mousetrap somewhere, even a mouse trying to get free of a trap, slapping it across a distant floor. A foot-
step, the sound of breathing? The sound of a cart on the tracks,
as if someone was pushing it down the tunnel or a wind was
somehow blowing underground? He would stand, wait, listen.
He would walk to the door of the tunnel, open it, stick his head
through. Silence.

◆

Colville picked up Kilo in one arm and climbed up the narrow
ladder to the lookout. Finally they reached the top, and he pushed
the dog in, climbed over, struggled to the long, low window.

There was still light outside, fading. Thick snowflakes fell,
white slanting through gray. The room around them was five feet
square, its ceiling low. Levers on the wall slapped open other,
smaller windows—only inches across, enough for the barrel of
a gun—and freezing air rushed in before he snapped them shut
again. There was one swiveling office chair here, and an old copy
of *Soldier of Fortune* magazine, hundreds of dead flies on the
floor.

Last night he'd heard footsteps, or sounds like footsteps. Faint
laughter that sounded almost like wind, that was likely only wind.
Little things—his multitool, his maps—migrated from the pack
while he slept, ended up on shelves or desktops. Sometimes he'd
return to his family's quarters and the floor would be open when
he was sure he'd slid the plywood cover back across. All he could
do was notice these things, and prepare himself, and wait.

Back down the ladder, he found his way to the classroom. The
secret wall, the hidden door. Every few hours, several times a day,
he came here, and each time he made some progress. Soon, he
would be able to withstand this energy, meet it with his own.

Bending down now, he crawled beneath the table of the altar.

He felt the waves, pressure in his ears, a slight pulse in his bones. He leaned in, laid his hand flat against the trembling door. He had never touched the lock, and now — for only a moment — he held it in his hand. Hot, it shook his whole arm, twisted his shoulder. He let go, stumbled to his feet. With Kilo close behind him, he hurried away, back toward the tunnel.

The trailer felt so temporary as a place to live, just as our bodies were temporary houses for our souls. Once in the kitchen I looked up and saw a mouse run across the clear plastic below the light, disappear into the ceiling. The window near the sink was bowed, plastic, scoured cloudy by the wind. Wings brushed softly in the walls, swallows making their way beneath the trailer's siding.

Maya and I slept. We woke up in the living room of the trailer, warm beneath our blankets on our mattress. We stayed in bed sometimes until Mom said we had to get up. Rarely we'd hear Dad as he left for the shelter, since he woke up so early. More often it was Mrs. Young with her morning decrees. Their altar was on the opposite side of ours, on the other side of the wool blanket and the bookcase, on their side of the living room. We could see movement, their bodies, in the gaps above the books, and we could hear them, their conversations, their footsteps. The whiskery clatter of the wires that Mr. Young carried, or the bitter smell and hiss when he was soldering something.

Mornings, the heavy wool blanket shook and trembled as if from the force of Mrs. Young's decrees, the energy of her breath forced out. She wanted the child she was carrying to be special, to come into the world with a lot of Light, and she was preparing the baby as it moved toward embodiment to join us in the physical plane. Maya and I just sat up in bed, listening, brushing each other's hair. Mrs. Young gasped, her voice circling, going so fast it was hard to see how she breathed. We listened, and we understood, or we thought we understood.

Now I can see, I can feel how she felt, wanting to do everything possible for the baby so it will be born healthy and happy, and lucky, so it will have the best life it can have. I don't sleep enough, now. I try to eat as healthy as I can. If I still believed, if I could believe like Mrs. Young did, I'd be decreeing all night, collecting pictures of gemstones, drawing double-helix diagrams of DNA, listening to waltzes, traveling in my dreams.

We had so many rules to guide us, our parents did, and now I wonder how I will raise you, what beliefs I have to pass down. Back then, everything was clear: you ate sugar, your energy fell; you listened to rock music, the bass and drums made your chakras spin backward. Christmas carols were always in season, filling a house with holiness. Stuffed animals were never allowed, and neither were comics where animals talked, or books by Dr. Seuss.

And then there were all the rules about food, the posters and diagrams hanging in our kitchen. The Messenger said that carrots were the only food that could grow at ten thousand feet, so they had to be right for us. We ate so many carrots that our skin was tinged orange.

14

It had been half an hour since she'd talked to the Messenger, and Francine's fingers, on the steering wheel, still trembled.

With the blue sky overhead, she drove down the long incline toward Livingston. She skipped the town and took the second exit. Past the McDonald's, the small shops of taxidermists and fishing guides. She drove south on 89, through the narrows, into Paradise Valley; the Yellowstone River flowed on the left, closer and then twisting away, returning. She passed a flatbed truck stacked high with hay bales, stalks and leaves fluttering across her windshield. She accelerated back into her lane and suddenly slowed again. Here was the turnoff to Mallard's Rest campground. Here her father's station wagon had gone straight into the river. He had been going in the other direction, north, in the other lane, just gone to pick something up in town.

That was almost twenty years ago, and it had been almost that long since she'd been in the valley. She hadn't come back; she hadn't been able to return. Not until this morning. The radio played static, humming higher and lower as she accelerated. She switched it off.

A new gas station had gone up across the street from the little town of Emigrant. The place itself looked almost the same: the post office, the saloon, all the haphazard houses of Glastonbury speckling the foothills behind it. Francine turned right, past the buildings and onto the gravel roads, then left, up the long switchbacks.

Writing about it hadn't fully prepared her for how beautiful it was, how broken. The makeshift cabins and the nicer ones, the dented trailers, the Airstreams, the pickup trucks, that blue sky everywhere pressing down on it all. Someone else might not recognize the bumps in the landscape like she did, the white hooked pipes that stuck out of the ground, ventilation for the shelters below, or recognize the half-hidden doors leading into the earth. The Kletter Shelter, Mark's Ark, all the ones whose names she'd forgotten.

Gravel rattled in her wheel wells, kicked up under the car. She had never driven here, had never been old enough; she lost her way, doubled back, found it again. Here the road leveled off and five trailers clustered. Ornate little houses stood against their outside walls. Someone else might believe they were dollhouses, or birdhouses. She knew they were for Elementals, and she wished she could feel the nature spirits now, helping her, invisible, all around her.

She parked, climbed out, then turned and walked away from her car, up the road. Already she was out of breath; she'd take the longer way, which was less steep. Helios Way, Capricorn Way, Sirius Way. These signs were new; these streets had never had names.

Higher, ahead, juniper trees hooked across the horizon. To the left, the plateau where their trailer had been, now completely bare. No triangle cut the air of the narrow canyon, the tepee long gone. She closed her eyes, shivered, then kept on, following the long curve around. She could see her car below, waiting where she'd left it, and now someone was watching her. She could feel it. Not from behind her, where she had been. It was from one of the houses she passed, set back in the limestone cliffs.

There. A two-story house, fifty feet away. Two people in different windows, upstairs and down, looking out. Who lived here, whose house had it been? Perhaps they recognized her.

Smoke sifted, blown sideways out the top of the chimney. The house was dark blue, its door pale yellow with three diamond-shaped windows. A blue Ford pickup with one black door stood parked to one side. Francine stepped past the mailbox, down the gravel driveway; halfway to the house, she looked up again and the faces were still there in the windows, watching her, so motionless that she realized they weren't people at all. They were posters pressed against the windowpanes, and there was a reason they looked familiar: El Morya with his turban, his black beard, his stern glaring eyes, and, in the upstairs window, Saint Germain beaming down.

Turning again, she climbed back to the road, around the last corner. She paused, her hands around her belly, her heart beating so fast. She tried to breathe, to slow it.

She turned off on a path she knew, worn down through the scrub as it arced along the side of a rise. The slope grew steeper; stones kicked loose, rolled downhill. She paused, rested, took another step, two. Her lungs held so little air, compressed by the baby. Then she went around the last corner, onto the small plateau.

The black metal door was set into the hump of the hillside, framed by railroad ties. A short square tunnel to reach it, and then the door with all its hinges on the inside, its three dead bolts. She unbuttoned, unzipped her pants, squatted down out of the wind, and peed between two clumps of sagebrush; then she stepped into the dark tunnel, to the door. It took a moment before she found the key Maya had given her — it was still too early for Maya to catch her, to catch up with her, to meet her — then to force the key into the stubborn locks. Slowly the dead bolts loosened, gave way. Still the door scraped; it took all of her weight to get it open enough to slip through into the darkness.

The tunnel continued, the dirt floor slanting downward. She waved her hand in the cool air above her head; spider webs against her fingers, then a string. When she pulled it, the walls around her flickered, the air bluish. Two fire extinguishers, a shovel, a camping lantern. The one long fluorescent bulb ticked and hummed overhead.

A twinge, a painful tightness in her stomach. Francine almost sat down. She waited, settled, then walked ten feet to the wooden handrail and went carefully down the steps.

Not so large as the outside door, this one was covered in huge rivets, two dead bolts locking it. In the dim light it took a while to fit the key in, to force the door open. She pushed with her knee, and then slapped around the corner with her hand, flipping on every light switch she could reach. She was inside.

Straight across the hallway from the door hung a poster of Cyclopea, the all-seeing eye, greeting her, staring. Watching over or just watching her. Next to it a framed portrait, the usual one, of Saint Germain. Water and insects had gotten inside the glass, so the left side of his face was pale and wrinkled, tattered, half of his blond mustache worn away. None of it seemed to bother him. He gazed out, reassuringly, as handsome and serene as ever, as if he didn't mind being buried here for so long.

Francine turned right, followed the curve of the hallway, stepped around mousetraps, boxes of rat poison torn and spilled open. It was warmer here, out of the wind; the air pressed close around her. It smelled more like dirt than she remembered. When it was all new, it had smelled like sweet wood, new lumber. It had hardly felt like being underground.

She passed the kitchen, the light flickering, all the chairs and tables stacked on top of each other. Huge pans hung from hooks in the curve of the ceiling. She kept going as the hallway narrowed, past the first numbered rooms.

There were thirty of them, thirty families. And when she reached the door with the brass 7 on it, she paused and could not quite stop. She was not ready. Not yet.

She kept walking, following the hallway's curve. Overhead, round openings, the inlets for the vacuum system that would spit dust and dirt back out into the world; beneath her feet, larger capped openings, which led to all the grain and food storage below.

Here, long shelves of books, covered in clear plastic; here, a treadmill, a weight bench; here, startling her, radiation suits hanging like white bodies from their racks.

The silence felt thick, pressurized, black in her ears. When she whistled, the sound echoed and followed the hallway all the way around, returning behind her. This was where her father had taught her, one day when the shelter was almost complete, with no one else inside. She was running around and around the circle of the hallway, doors and numbers flashing past. Her father's whistling echoed down the tube; she could hear it from the other side, where she couldn't see him. And then she whistled and it echoed to him, and he whistled back to her.

She whistled again. The faint sound that returned to her made her feel better; as if it were more than her own breath.

Next she came to a short metal ladder, bolted to the inside wall, which led to the lookout, the periscope where she and Colville had once played. Another twinge, sharp in her stomach, a shifting ache inside. What time was it? She had no watch, didn't have her cell phone to tell her the time or to call anyone. Did Maya say she was definitely coming? Francine waited, let her body settle, her breathing slow.

Number 7. She passed their room again. At number 4, she tried the door, stepped inside, flipped on the light. Nothing except bed frames. No mattresses or clothes or books left behind. This had been Colville's family's room, before the Messenger called them away to the shelter at the Heart.

Francine sat on the lower bunk, which must have been for Colville. His name was written on the wall, in pencil, the graphite reflecting the light. Next to it, a few small flying saucers were scratched, hovering over a kind of figure. She leaned closer. It was a person with long hair, an enormous belly. She sat up at once, hit her head on the bunk above, then realized that it was not supposed to be her, that Colville hadn't been here for years and years. The drawing was of Colville's mother, of course; Mrs. Young had been expecting Colville's little brother back then. Moses.

Francine returned to the kitchen, took a chair from the top of a table. She sat down, closed her eyes. It made her so happy, and it also made her so tired. All the work and then all the years after, this space becoming so empty and lonesome and misguided. It would feel different if it had been used, if the bombs had come. And then her parents might still be here.

◆

Footsteps, descending the stairs, and then the slight creak as the door opened.

Maya's voice called: "Hello?"

"Down here," Francine said. "The kitchen." She stood, brushed back her hair, felt the tangles, the sticky spider webs. Maya walked toward her, into darkness, under a light again, back into shadow. She wore her heavy boots, her tan Carhartt jacket, her hair pulled back in a messy ponytail.

"You all right?" she said.

"I was resting."

"Your face is dirty. You look terrible."

"It's dirty in here." Francine took the bottle of water Maya held out.

"So many things," Maya said, "when you're growing up, you go back and they look so miniature. But this place still feels so big." She looked past Francine, down the hallway. "You've already been through our room?"

Francine twisted the cap onto the bottle, handed it back. "I was waiting for you."

They headed along the hallway, the brass numbers on the doors counting up.

"You didn't have to wait."

120

"I know."

"Couldn't go in alone?"

Maya opened the door, holding it so Francine could squeeze past, inside. There was the click of the light switch. The darkness remained.

"Hold on." Maya brushed past, swore as she unscrewed a light bulb in the hallway. Returning, she passed the hot bulb from hand to hand. She stood on the edge of the bunk, her hand on Francine's shoulder.

The room flickered as she screwed in the bulb tight. Brighter and brighter, the blue spines and red stripes, the gold numbers of the encyclopedias, the dusty framed photographs, the bare mattresses chewed by mice, cotton batting pulled loose onto the floor.

"Here we are," Francine said.

"This room actually does feel smaller than I remember." Maya pointed to Francine's bunk, perched above the door. "And that would have fit you for how long? It's tiny."

Francine squinted upward. The two dark knotholes in the ceiling were still there, staring down at her. She looked away, bent over to reach for an empty plastic bucket with a lid. Sitting on it, she pulled out a box from under the bed, opened it. Shoes, sneakers and leather boots, growing in size from left to right, from 6 to 11.

"You would've been wearing my hand-me-downs the whole time," Maya said. "Seven years of them."

"I did, anyway."

Maya brushed off the mattress, then lay down on her side, cradling her head on one arm. "Did you go downstairs?"

"No," Francine said.

"That's the part that always gets me. Those little desks and chairs, the way Mom painted those windows onto the walls so it seemed like you could see outside. The sun, the trees, the river. What are you looking for?"

"Nothing," Francine said. "Just looking." She pulled out a plastic box that held socks, balled up tightly in pairs; shoelaces, sorted by length and color; fingernail and toenail clippers. She pulled out a sheepskin jacket, then a pale blue sweater with a glittery horse on the front.

"Beautiful," Maya said. "Awful." She rolled over, staring up at the slats of the bunk above. "I don't know, Francine. It's just — it's always like this. Every couple years I come back down here, have a cry, and then I'm good for a while. It's the classroom that gets me, all the Montessori shit, the felt board and sandpaper letters, all of Mom's work. Dad, he was having a great time. He always said it was like building a big fort. He could really see it that way. He could make people believe."

Francine turned her back, shifting herself off the plastic bucket to the floor. Opening a cabinet, she found pads of blank paper, piles of documents, envelopes with writing on them. She checked behind her; beneath the shadow of the bed, it was hard to tell if Maya was watching. Then her sister picked up a framed picture from the bedside table, held it to her face. Francine carefully pried the lid from the bucket, slipped some of the papers inside. Next, a notebook with her name on the cover in her mother's perfect cursive. She slipped in a knit scarf, a pair of mittens connected by a length of yarn.

Maya set the framed picture back on the table. It was a photograph of their grandparents.

"I remember that night," she said, "thinking about all the people like Grandma and Grandpa we'd left behind because they were on the outside and didn't understand how things were. I remember thinking about all the beautiful places I'd been to that wouldn't be there anymore."

"You were so upset about your friend, Courtney," Francine said. "That's what I remember."

"What are you doing with that bucket? What are you putting in there?"

"I thought, for the baby, I'd take a few things. Maybe clothes that were meant for me, my baby would use them."

"I think you should leave those things here," Maya said.

"What?"

"Mom and Dad put them here. I don't know."

"It's not getting used down here," Francine said. "It never will."

"Still. That's how I feel."

Francine looked away, at the line of encyclopedias on the shelf, the textbooks and notebooks, the books about the impressionists and King Arthur.

"I talked to Wells this morning," Maya said.

"What?"

"I called your cell and he picked up. You left it behind."

"You told him I was here?"

"If you'd told me he didn't know," Maya said, "that you didn't want him to know. You told me you'd call him —"

"It doesn't matter, really."

"He asked if you were alone."

"Alone?" She imagined Wells, alone in the house, holding her phone, asking Maya all these questions.

"Francine?" Maya said. "What does that mean?"

"All I wanted was to come back here by myself," she said. "I didn't want to have to talk and explain all about it. I just did." Reaching for the bedpost, she pulled herself up, stood. "I think I'm ready to go now."

"You're sure?"

"I've been down here longer than you have."

"Okay." Maya swung her legs around, her feet on the floor, and stood up.

Francine followed her sister into the hallway. They closed the door with the brass 7 nailed to it, then walked through the kitchen, switching off lights as they went. Under the gaze of Cyclopea, onto the steps of the antechamber with the bright sky framed above, ahead the sound of wind. Francine climbed toward them.

"Key?" Maya said, behind her.

"What?"

"Do you have it?"

"Here."

Francine went ahead. She held the plastic bucket in front of her, where Maya wouldn't see it, even if Maya had already seen it.

Outside again, the day felt colder, the wind sharper, and the sun not so bright. The truck was parked next to the shelter; Maya had driven it off the road, through the scrub.

"I brought you a sandwich," she said. "I figured you'd need it."

"I do."

The sisters sat in the truck's cab, out of the wind, looking through the windshield at the wide valley spread out below. The highway, the river, thin clouds blowing past.

Maya wiped at her mouth, then set her sandwich on the dashboard. She reached into her jacket pocket, held out her phone.

"What?"

"You should call home."

"Later. I'll do it."

"You want me to go outside so you can talk?" Maya opened her door; the wind whistled everywhere, blowing napkins around the cab. "Here."

"No," Francine said. "Really. I don't want to, right now. Not here."

Maya slammed the door, slouched down. "It's not like you can keep them separate," she said.

"What?"

"It's not like you can come back here and solve it and leave it behind, then go back and start your family or whatever. It's all connected — all this, and you, and what you're doing now, and Wells, the baby, everything."

"I'm not saying —"

"How do you think Wells feels?"

"I just wanted to come back for a day or two. It doesn't have to be that big a deal." Francine stared out at the rickety blue and purple houses below, at the cars on the highway, the dark river, and, far away on Emigrant Peak, the pattern of trees and snow that still looked like a seahorse. "Didn't you ever do something without knowing why?" she said.

"Are you talking about coming back here? Or everything you've done since you left?"

"I'm just asking you a question."

"Sometimes," Maya said. "Sometimes I do what I want or have to even though I know it's hurting someone, and then later I say I couldn't help myself, or I had no control over it."

"That's different."

"Is it?"

Frowning, Maya turned in her seat and faced Francine. "You, you moved away. You didn't come back. That was smart, in a way. I'm reminded all the time — places, people. You need a plumber or electrician, half the contractors in town are ex-members, people who came to work on the shelters. It's crazy-making. It's how we grew up, I know, but still. If you think too much about it, you can get either really confused or really angry."

"I like to think about it, though," Francine said. "Sometimes, I think that was the happiest I've been."

"When you were ten? Of course you were happy."

"You sound mad," Francine said.

"I'm not mad."

"When I think about it, sometimes I feel just the same as I did, then."

"Sometimes," Maya said, "when I'm stressed at work, or I'm driving in a snowstorm, I'll hear my voice decreeing, saying the Archangel Michaels, and I can't even stop myself. I hate that, like it's inside me, just waiting."

She fished the key from her pocket and started the truck,

shifted into gear. They jerked across the plateau, back onto the road and down the slope, toward where Francine's car was parked. The only sound was the gravel beneath the tires.

"I wish we didn't have two cars," Maya said, "that you didn't have to drive all the way back to Bozeman."

"I'm not."

"What?"

"I'm not going back with you."

"What?"

"I'm headed home."

"That's too far. Francine, sleep over, then start out in the morning."

"I'll get a room at Chico, tonight, or down in Gardiner, and then tomorrow I'll go back through Yellowstone. It's shorter that way."

"If the road's still open." Maya pulled over, next to Francine's car.

"Thanks for coming," Francine said. "It helped."

"Call me tomorrow. Let me know you're home all right. Here, give me a hug."

Francine climbed down, then reached into the bed of the truck and lifted out the white plastic bucket. She stood beside her car, watching the brake lights of Maya's truck blink as they rounded the curve and dropped out of sight. The truck reappeared, after a moment, going down the switchback below, and was gone again.

15

IN THE LOBBY of Chico Hot Springs resort, children ran back and forth, screaming; they wore bathing suits, clutched white towels, disappeared down shadowed hallways. A fire burned, casting shadows from the hearth. Out the windows, the afternoon had turned cold and dark.

Francine stood at the desk, checking in. This was all so much fancier than she remembered, from back when she had come to the hot springs as a girl. She held her white plastic bucket in one hand, the papers almost weightless inside it, its lid snapped on tight. A man in a red mackinaw walked past, smiled. He seemed familiar; this kept happening, as if someone might suddenly know her, as if everyone knew her and she could not quite recognize them.

Upstairs, her room had ruffles on the bed and the curtains. Small and cozy, it might have been decorated by a pioneer wife. She kicked off her clogs, set down the bucket. She pressed her forehead to the cold window, looked up a slope to where a ramshackle A-frame stood, where right now someone could be looking down, might see her pale face. Below the A-frame, black pipes snaked down the hillside, forked this way and that, went underground and resurfaced again as they brought hot water from the springs.

Drawing the curtains, she turned, brushed her teeth in the bathroom, set a glass of water on the bedside table. Then, before she climbed into bed, she pried the lid from the white bucket. She set the small pile of papers on her pillow.

The first paper was folded three times, and she opened it to reveal a cross-section of their shelter's construction. Her father's handwriting, in red ink, pointed out changes in the ventilation system, detailed the steps of the backfill, how to bury the whole thing without crushing it. She folded the plans away. Next were two watercolors, their paper rigid with dried paint: one by Maya, of a horse standing beneath a tree; another by Francine, her age (7) in the sky next to a sun that shone down on a girl whose smile stretched beyond the edges of her face.

The next sheet of paper was official stationery. It was old, the address in Malibu, before the move to Montana. It took a moment for Francine to understand it, though there were only three lines: a letter from the Messenger to her parents, either telling them that they must marry or giving their marriage her blessing.

A blue envelope held a card with a picture of a sunset on it. It was from her grandparents, to her parents, saying, *You have our love even if we cannot be with you, even if we cannot agree. We appreciate your prayers and welcome them even if we do not understand.*

Next was a love note from her father to her mother, dated 1979, that she couldn't quite bring herself to read. Not yet. And then the last piece of paper, at the bottom of the pile: another letter from the Messenger, a more recent one. It was from 1981.

```
Hello My Daughter,
    I have been thinking of you and your family,
Dearest Loving Hearts Who Keep the Flame of Life
on Earth. Some Keepers of the Flame in the field
have told me they are waiting for a signal be-
fore they plan on taking any action in terms of
survival. This is not the case with you and your
family, for which I am glad and for which the
Masters are glad.
```

Blessed heart, I have several letters from
you here and must respond all at once. As for
reports of Maya's disobedience: I remind you
that she is still a very young girl, and harsh
measures will not avail you. Say the Heart, Head
and Hand decrees with her before she goes to bed
at night. Decree for her, yourself. Decree the
Tube of Light over her while she sleeps.

Most importantly, congratulations on welcom-
ing a new soul into your family! I am in agree-
ment that Francine is a fine name, and you have
my blessing to use it for your daughter. Already
I can tell that she has lived important lives in
previous embodiments, and has returned to us for
a reason. Your daughter will be the mother of a
daughter of great Light indeed.
All my Love forever,
Mother
P.S. You will soon receive (or may already have
received) a mailing concerning our Royal Teton
Food Storage Program. We are offering a compre-
hensive food program for survival created by our
staff of food-production professionals and nu-
trition consultants. It includes organic grains,
beans, and vegetables, many of which are grown
right here on the ranch, and optional meat and
dairy. Our food units are for sale only to reg-
istered Communicants.

Francine set down the sheet of paper. She went into the bathroom, peed one last time, washed her hands. Carefully she then
set the papers back in the bucket, unwound the scarf from her
neck. She closed her eyes, drifted toward sleep.

◆

In the morning, it took a moment to remember where she was.
The scarf on the bedpost, the bucket on the floor. When she

opened the curtains, the windows were frosted over; she shivered, closed them again, pulled on her clothes.

Downstairs in the lobby, the fire was burning, and people were sitting around the hearth with newspapers and laptops, drinking coffee from paper cups. The buffet was not yet open; the door to the dining room was locked. Francine turned and went back up the stairs, down the hallway, following the arrows on the walls, past her own room. At the bottom of a narrow stairway, she pushed open the door.

Steam was everywhere, rising from the hot water in the long pool into the dark sky overhead. Was anyone here? It was impossible to say. She stepped out of her clogs and felt the coldness of the concrete through her stocking feet.

Voices. She squinted: a man and a woman with a baby floating in an inflatable ring. The baby laughed, splashed, disappeared into the clouds of steam.

Francine took off her socks, rolled up her pant legs. She sat on the edge of the pool, easing her feet down into the hot water. When she was a girl, this had been one of the special places, one of the rare times they were out in the world with other people, people who weren't members of the Activity. They were more exposed than at any other time, even if they weren't allowed to wear bathing suits; they wore long shorts, knee socks, tights. She remembered how exciting it had been to splash along through the thick steam, uncertain whether the other children around her, their faces hard to see, were people she knew. She remembered the touch of skin underwater, of fingers suddenly around her ankle and suddenly gone. At night there were lights over the pool; she would float on her back in the hot water and stare up at the edge of the darkness, the stars.

"Good morning," a woman said. "A beautiful one."

"Yes," Francine said.

The woman wore a flowered bathing cap and had two long, wet white braids on her shoulders; she plowed through the water, running in slow motion. After a moment she returned, coming through the steam.

"Cold out," she said.

"My butt's freezing," Francine said.

"So get in."

"Can't," she said. "I don't have a suit. And I'm not supposed to. The hot water."

"When are you due?"

"Five weeks. A little more than a month."

The water magnified the woman's lower body, made her legs seem to bend away at an odd angle. She kicked them, circled her arms, going through a series of motions. Exercises. She continued to look at Francine, not moving away. Her earlobes stuck out the bottom of her cap; small turquoise studs shone there.

"You're Francine, aren't you?"

"That's my name, yes."

The woman laughed. "You don't look so different from when you were a little girl. Your face. I knew you then. I knew your parents. I'm Juliet Stiller."

"Mrs. Stiller," Francine said. "Courtney's mom."

"I know, I don't look the same. I'm old! I have to come down here almost every morning for my arthritis."

More voices. Bodies leapt into the water, colored suits flashed here and there. Francine felt wetness on her head; she looked up and cold flakes landed on her face.

"It's snowing."

"It is."

"I was thinking back," Francine said. "How we used to come here."

"Yes — I remember times when Courtney was a teenager that I tried to keep her away, but of course that didn't work."

Francine kicked her legs gently, felt the cold where her calves were wet, above the surface of the hot water. She looked down, then up at Mrs. Stiller again.

"How is Courtney?"

"She's down in California—Oakland—with her girlfriend, now." Mrs. Stiller held a long, blue foam tube under her arms; she straightened one leg so her toes broke the surface of the water, then the other. "She comes back a couple times a year, tells me how wrong I am about everything."

Francine tried to remember what had happened to Courtney, after she disappeared, after that night in the shelter. She was really Maya's friend. Had she come back? Had she stayed away?

"She's my daughter," Mrs. Stiller said. "The only one I have. Have to love her—you'll see how it is when you have your daughter." Now she splashed with her hands, drifting farther away, closer again. "I like the cold snowflakes and the hot water together," she said. "Don't you?"

"Yes."

"I saw you yesterday." Mrs. Stiller swung her arms wide, then together in front of her, just under the surface of the water. "Did I say that? Your old place is gone, of course."

"Yes."

"Looked like you went up to the shelter."

"To think if we'd lived down there, all those years," Francine said. "If we hadn't been wrong—"

"Were we wrong?" Mrs. Stiller sank lower in the water, blew bubbles, rose again. "No one knows what would've happened if we hadn't built the shelters. We were trying to survive and we did survive, and now there's a world out here, still a place where Light can be gathered. And I've never been with so many creative, determined folks working in the same direction. Never before, never since."

"You're still involved?"

"With the Activity? Oh, no." Mrs. Stiller laughed. "Not exactly. After the Messenger, without her it became more like a publishing company, really—no real leader, none of the people we knew. No one down in Corwin Springs is really practicing like we did—and you know, what happened to the Messenger, the loss of her, that was more startling than the world not ending."

As she listened to Mrs. Stiller, as clouds of steam pressed down all around her, Francine tried to concentrate on the wetness of the water, the cold concrete beneath her. The snowflakes seemed to come down hot, like cinders, cooling slowly on her skin. The water around her legs felt cold. Icy. She reached her hands in, splashed her face, held her cold fingers over the sockets of her eyes.

"Are you feeling all right?" Mrs. Stiller said. "Any cramping?"

"Why?" Francine said. "Why did you say I would have a daughter?"

"Did I say that?"

"Just now."

"I don't remember."

"You did say it."

"You were friends with the Youngs' boy," Mrs. Stiller said. "I remember you running around together. I remember seeing your two blond heads, way up in the canyons."

"Colville," Francine said. "I saw him not long ago."

"You must have had a lot to talk about, plenty of memories."

"Yes."

"I wonder," Mrs. Stiller said. "Would you join us this afternoon? A few friends of mine—we meet at my house around three o'clock."

"I don't know if I'll still be here, later today."

"Think about it. No, don't think—see how you feel. We study the Teachings, decree, raise our voices together, listen to taped dictations. My house, you know which one it is. A yellow door, the diamond-shaped windows. Even yesterday I could see all your energy, all the Light inside you. I can feel it now."

"I'll think about it," Francine said. "Right now, I'm freezing."

"Of course. Go inside now, dear. Eat something. Drink something warm."

◆

The hearth was slightly rounded, of polished stone; a broken wagon wheel was etched high above the flames. Francine sat watching the fire, her feet up near the metal grate. She ate a bowl of oatmeal, sipped at lemon tea. She imagined how it would be, if she went to Mrs. Stiller's house. Would she remember the decrees; would she be able to keep up? The speed of the voices had always risen to a hum, like insects vibrating, leaving hardly time or space to breathe. A swarm of words. Perhaps the decrees would return, the Teachings still inside her, waiting to be brought into practice, to surface.

A man with bifocals and a gray mustache sat across from her, reading the *New York Times*. He kept glancing up, as if about to say something; she'd noticed this, the friendliness of strangers since she'd been pregnant, her pregnancy a reason to engage her. It was a little like walking a dog, how it brought strangers close. She thought for a moment of Kilo, either circling the back yard or asleep under the kitchen table. Or maybe Wells had started to let the dog sleep on the bed, since she'd been gone. Wells, worrying now, wondering. Francine laid a hand flat on her belly, her shirt warm from the fire. *Your daughter will be the mother of a daughter of great Light indeed.* To think that the woman who wrote that was now the woman feeding apples to horses, the path from one to another running at the same time as Francine traveled around the canyons as a girl, in and out of the shelter and away, far away, to another life, until here she was again, circling back, a person with a person inside her.

How would I even go about teaching you, being a mother in that way? Perhaps I would tell you to think of yourself as a radio station, sending forth good thoughts, peace and goodwill. Would that be too much? Would I believe it? Perhaps I will ask that you tell your mind to act with decision, alertness and quickness, not to waver; when you have a sudden feeling to do a certain constructive thing, stick to it and do it, whatever the outcome. That is something that the Messenger taught us, and I would like to believe it, to be able to act without wavering. I would like to believe that we are not these lower bodies, but that we are beings using these vehicles to accomplish an end. I will say, I will tell you that whatever happens, don't make matters worse because you're afraid of looking foolish. I will say to forgive yourself, to forgive others, to learn while your body sleeps.

16

WELLS STOOD in the middle of the living room with the pages Francine had written in his hands. It was morning again, and the only light came from the windows, the whiteness outside, the snow still drifting down. A day had passed, and Francine was still not home, had still not called.

A loose page glowed white, under the couch, catching the light from the window. Wells bent down to pick it up, then went into the kitchen and set the pages in a ragged pile on the counter, next to the phone. He called Maya — at home, at work, on her cell; he listened to the ringing, the recorded greetings, but he did not leave a message. As he listened, he shuffled through the pages: Francine playing with Colville in the broken foundation of an old cabin, long grass torn out for beds; chanting at a forest fire; falling from a tall tree and not being hurt; passages of reflection, explanation.

> When I tell people I grew up in Montana, they start talking about cowboys and ranches, when for me it had nothing to do with that. It was the world and the universe, the visible and the invisible, not a state in a country. I had chosen the family I was born into, and I was here for a reason, and it was a matter of living up to the path I was born with.

At the sink, he splashed cold water on his face, then started the coffeemaker, listened to its cough and hiss. Cold wind blew in when he opened the side door, just long enough to glance at the empty driveway.

He wasn't hungry, but he toasted a piece of bread, drank a glass of milk. The phone book lay open on the counter. He had been thinking of calling the animal shelters, to check for Kilo. A black dog, medium-sized, wearing a leather collar. Was that too vague a description? He picked up the phone, set it down. If Francine called while he was dialing, would she get a busy signal? He didn't call. Instead, he set his empty glass in the sink and went back down the hallway, into the baby's room.

There were no more documents to find on the computer, nothing hidden or new. Sitting at the desk, he slowly cycled through photographs of their honeymoon, up in the Sawtooths, along the Salmon River. Francine, the fine blond hairs of her arms catching the sun. The braid on one side of her head had come undone. Kilo lay in a patch of sunlight behind her, raising his head to snap at a fly. Far below, a bright green lake, looking so cold and deep, in the crater of an extinct volcano; beyond that, the ragged edge of the mountains. They'd joked about the Sawtooths, about turning the whole range over, sawing the world in two. Later they'd counted the mile markers, found the hot springs, close to the highway, along the river. Wells had had poison oak, so he couldn't get in the hot water; instead, he stood watching Francine throw her clothes to one side and scrabble along the riverbank, the full moon shining down on her broad white back. Headlights wheeled suddenly overhead, cars and trucks on the highway, so close. He told her he'd stand there, warn her if someone was coming. *What are they going to do?* she'd said. *See me naked?*

The phone rang from the kitchen; he stumbled to his feet, tripped on the computer cord.

It was only Stuart from work, wondering if he was coming in.

"I should've called," Wells said. "It's my wife and everything, you know, the baby — no, it's not here, not yet."

"That's fine," Stuart said. "It's slow in here anyway, what with the weather."

Wells hung up the phone, wiped the toast crumbs from the counter. In his peripheral vision then he saw motion — a dark shape out in the street. It was the neighbor girl, on her bike. Sliding, kicking up snow behind her, she cut back and forth, the light blue of her coat and her bright yellow hat surrounded by all that whiteness.

Dialing quickly, he called all three of Maya's numbers again. She wasn't at work, no one knew why, and there was no one at her house, and she didn't answer her cell phone.

He could not sit still. He circled the house, sweeping floors, straightening furniture. His cell phone in one pocket, Francine's in the other. The bright snow shone in through the windows.

When he passed through the kitchen, he slowed, read a page or two again, thought of them as he circled. He liked to imagine Francine doing all these things, a girl so long ago. And reading about her parents — it was as if he were finally meeting them, and they were the same age as he was now.

He paused. A car in the driveway? A car door opening, slamming shut? Footsteps? No. Had this house always creaked like this?

> Colville said snow insulates sound, which makes it hard to hear anyone following and also makes it harder for them to hear us. I asked him how come sound carries across water and he said that snow is frozen, that it doesn't weigh as much.

Wells read in the sharp light that slanted in through the window. He read about Colville's parents, practicing survival skills, setting up a lean-to of sticks with a silver foil blanket over the top, a shelter that fit across the mouth of a cave.

A knocking, a soft knocking. He slid a little in his stocking feet as he turned the corner, into the living room.

When he pulled the front door open, no one was there. Cold wind blew in, and there were footprints in the snow, and something — he bent down to pick it up; it was Kilo's leather collar, the metal tags jangling — and then the neighbor girl running away, back toward her house, her dark hair now loose.

"Hey!" he said. "Wait!"

The phone was ringing again. He hurried backward, inside; Kilo's collar, stiff and cold, was still in his hand as he picked up the phone, as he listened.

"Wells," Maya said. "You need to be here. You need to get here as fast as you can."

Standing there in the kitchen, listening, he watched snow drift through the open front door, collecting white on the hardwood floor of the living room.

On All Saints' Day we dressed up as Ascended Masters, as Sylphs and Undines and Salamanders, all the Elementals. We paraded in front of the Messenger and she announced the best costume. The men built special rooms to look like the retreats of the Masters. They took one of the rooms in the shelter and covered all the walls and ceilings and floor with pink insulation, so it was like a strange cloud. We couldn't have sugar, so we didn't get any candy. That year of the shelters, the men carved these little hearts out of rosewood. Instead of candy we were given these perfectly smooth hearts to keep.

17

COLVILLE KNELT IN the darkness, before the small, hidden door. Stretching out the heavy bolt cutters, he took hold of the padlock between the pincers and squeezed. The lock dropped to the plywood floor with a heavy, hollow knock.

He moved backward a few feet, waited to see what would happen, if the door would open by itself. Then he closed his eyes, did his visualizations, and began to decree:

> *"Beloved I AM Presence bright,*
> *Round me seal your Tube of Light*
> *From Ascended Master flame*
> *Called forth now in God's own name.*
> *Let me keep my temple free*
> *From all discord sent to me.*
> *I AM calling forth Violet Fire*
> *To blaze and transmute all desire,*
> *Keeping on in Freedom's name*
> *Till I AM one with the Violet Flame."*

He opened his eyes, took a long breath, exhaled slowly. Then, on his hands and knees, he eased himself forward.

The door scraped as he pulled it open. Darkness, silence, the smell of mildew. He switched on his headlamp, crawled through; he ran his hands along the floor to each wall, the space only a few feet square. He reached up and felt nothing. He tilted his head, the light's beam, and saw the ceiling ten feet overhead.

As he lifted his hand from the floor to kneel, he felt something else — a shelf, two steps. To his right, almost behind him, were two, three wooden steps and a small, porchlike landing. He turned around, the beam of his headlamp shining on a door, a purple door that looked like it belonged on a Victorian house. He stood, climbed the stairs. The door had a brass knocker shaped like a fist bolted to its middle, and a round glass peephole, and two heavy padlocks bolted above its knob.

Colville backed down the steps. As he turned, bending to reach back through the tiny door for the bolt cutters, he saw light in his peripheral vision: a round spot of light in the darkness. He switched off his headlamp, turned to face the purple door again. Light shone through the peephole; the same flickering, bluish light lined the bottom of the door.

He cut the locks, set them gently on the floor.

"Kilo," he said.

Colville knelt, but the dog only whined, backing up, lying down again with his head resting on his paws.

"Fine. Stay behind, then." He pushed open the purple door and stood still for a moment, his eyes adjusting to the lights, the long fluorescent tubes humming in the low ceiling. Then he took one step inside and paused, uncertain whether he should go farther. Silence; he felt buffeted, as if he were standing close to a huge machine, an engine of some kind pounding the air.

The room was almost fifteen feet square, and it was a bedroom. He stood next to a queen-size bed, a four-poster with a pale violet comforter resting on top of its mattress. A bookshelf along one wall, the bed, bedside tables holding framed photographs of children. He stepped closer; he recognized the children — they were the Messenger's sons and daughters. This was her room, where she would have been safe, planning for the future, consulting with the Masters.

For a moment he felt the weight of the forty feet of earth overhead, felt how these rooms without windows seemed to contract. He slowed his breathing. Inhaled, exhaled. As his eyes adjusted to the brightness of the lights, his body adjusted to the pressure in the air. He walked around the bed and his footsteps echoed, the built-up floor hollow beneath him. Storage.

A long desk ran along the back wall. Atop it, two old computers hummed; green and red lines, still visible through the dust, bounced across their screens. Dust covered the papers, too, and mouse droppings, tiny footprints. A pile of mimeographed decree inserts were stacked to one side; he read the top one: *I demand a bolt of lightning into the cause and core of the beast of sensuality dominating the motion pictures of this year as well as the beast of horror and violence in The Alien, Prophecy, Nightwings, Dracula, The Amityville Horror, Dawn of the Dead, Halloween, Phantasm, Nosferatu, The Shining, Love at First Bite.*

Further down the desk, a gnawed yellow pencil rested on a sheet of paper that was covered with flowing handwriting:

> *It might seem like a paradox that our Activity, so set on ascending beyond this earth, escaping this material plane, would work so hard to stay alive and in our bodies, on this earth. The thing you must understand is that we need this world to do our work, to transmute darkness to Light. We need a place to stand while we do this. It's the same as the way our souls need our bodies, as a temporary place to reside. The Masters reminded us of this. In 1982, Saint Germain himself said that the ancient manuscripts of another world prophesied that the victory of the cosmos would unfold on our planet. This is the struggle that we're engaged in, that we're leading.*

A sound. A scratching at the door. Turning, Colville crossed the room and let Kilo in. The dog sneezed, then entered gingerly.

He circled as if he would bite his tail, around three times, almost settled, then moved over by the desk, circled four more times, and finally collapsed with a sigh.

Colville stepped close to the bookcase. Here were photos of the Messenger; frames also held images of Marie Antoinette, Nefertiti, Queen Guinevere — some of the Messenger's earlier embodiments. Here, too, were the green books of the I AM activity, and volumes about theosophy, and plenty written by the Messenger herself.

On the lowest shelf, tinfoil caught the light, wrapped around something the size of a toolbox. He knelt down, reaching out to touch it. Some of the silver came off against his finger; he realized that the foil had been wrapped around books — first individually, then seven or eight together. Carefully, he lifted them as one, almost set them on the floor, then swung them over to the bed, rested them on the comforter. The silver flaked away, brittle with age.

The Book of Black Magic and of Pacts, by Arthur Edward Waite; *Hypnotherapy,* by Dave Elman; *Necronimicon,* by Ed Simon; *The Satanic Bible,* by Anton LaVey; *Memoir on the Discovery of Animal Magnetism,* by Franz Mesmer.

Colville opened this last one, slowly, hearing the old glue of its spine crack. Scrawled across the endpapers, the same handwriting, in pencil: *I call for the legions of Archangel Michael. Lord Michael descend! Michael descend! Michael descend! We call for the flaming sword of blue flame. Encircle all demons. Encircle the fallen ones. Encircle the legions of darkness. BLAZE the light of Cyclopea. BLAZE through! Blue lightning bombs descend from the heart of Hercules.*

There was no dust on the comforter, nor on the bedside tables, which gleamed as if they had been oiled. There were sheets on the bed, starched white pillowcases. Colville realized he was crying, tears on his face. He closed the book, glanced over at Kilo just as the dog raised his head, ears up.

A knock, the metal sound of brass, three times.

Kilo leapt to his feet, tail wagging, and ran to the door.

Still on the bed, Colville watched the door, less than ten feet away. Dead bolts lined one edge; he hadn't locked them.

Now Kilo let out one happy bark, his tail cutting back and forth through the air.

Another knock. Silence.

Standing, moving as quietly as possible, Colville leaned close, squinted through the peephole. The light was so dim; all he could see was a dark silhouette. A man's shoulders and head, smooth hair, standing tall. And all at once the deep voice: "You're going to invite me in?"

Colville stepped back, almost tripping over Kilo.

"Are you going to open the door?"

"It's not locked." Colville reached out and swung it open.

"Hello, I'm dreaming," the man said, ducking slightly as he stepped into the room, squinting his bright blue eyes. Kilo leapt up, and the man bent to kiss the dog on his snout, to scratch behind his ears. Then he straightened again, smiled.

"Colville," he said. "Surely you're not surprised to see me?"

The man was tall, six foot four or five; the fluorescent lights were close to the top of his head, his blond hair shiny and solid-looking, darker at the roots. His beard, too, was blond, its edges sharp, comb marks visible in the whiskers. His eyes were so blue, unblinking, and he wore a white robe somewhere between a bathrobe and a karate outfit. Colville's mother's blue knit scarf around his neck. Barefoot.

"See you got into those books." The man laughed, waved one large hand to the bed, where the old tinfoil shone dull and cracked, ripped into fragments, the books scattered.

"I didn't mean to wreck anything."

"She did that." The man chuckled, scratching at his beard. "She did it to keep in all the vibrations; she wanted to know what was in there, but she wanted to control it, too." He glanced back at

Colville. "What? You're worried? She had plenty of crazy ideas. These books aren't going to hurt anyone." He smiled again. "Or at least tinfoil's not changing anything."

"The Messenger," Colville said, looking over at the framed portrait on the bookshelf, her steady eyes looking out.

"Don't get me wrong." The man pressed his hands flat against the ceiling as if holding it up, preventing the weight of the earth from crashing down on them. "She was a great messenger, but where once there was one, now there are many, and the highest Teachings are the ones inside us. The simple ones. You know that."

"I know who you are," Colville said.

"You were waiting for me, and here I am. Call me Jeremy." Crouching down, he scratched Kilo again, squinted up at Colville. "We'll have some fine travels together."

"Where?" Colville said.

"You don't trust me?" Jeremy chuckled again. "We'll travel light," he said. "I'll meet you in half an hour or so, back in the room where you've been sleeping. Then we'll set out."

"Come on, Kilo," Colville said, turning.

"Would you leave the dog with me?"

"I'd rather he came with me."

"As you like it," Jeremy said. "We'll all be together soon enough. Until then."

Colville crawled through the tiny door, led Kilo back to the tunnel. After helping the dog onto the cart, he wheeled him through the familiar darkness.

18

When colville climbed up the ladder, out of the cylinder, it was the middle of the day, the sun a pale disk through the clouds.

"Here," Jeremy said, pushing cloth bags into the orange frame pack. "Some of this dried fish you like, and some rice, and something for Kilo, too, of course."

The dog leapt sideways, excited at the sound of his name, attentive to Jeremy's every gesture.

"Where were you before?" Colville said.

"Before when?"

"Before you were here."

"Before? I was here, before. And I was elsewhere, too—always traveling." Kneeling, Jeremy now held two tubes of blue nylon with black rubber soles roughly sewn on, long black laces trailing. He stood barefoot in the snow, slapping ice from his feet before he slipped them into the boots.

"Moon boots," Colville said.

"Pardon me?"

"I remember them, from when I was a kid."

"Yes," Jeremy said. "I remember them as well." He pulled the laces tight, then stood, smiling. "Is something the matter?"

"No," Colville said.

"You seem troubled. What is it?"

"If you're a Master, if you're Saint Germain, how can I even stand so close to you? How come I can see you? Because I've gotten stronger?"

Jeremy laughed. "Wouldn't you think I could control my state of vibration, dial it down?" Now he stepped closer to the hatch; he reached down and lifted the cover on its hinge. When he let it go, it snapped shut with a hollow sound.

"Did you leave it open for me?" Colville said. "That first day?"

"I figured you could use a little help — of course, it won't do any good if I take all your tests for you."

Jeremy looked away, pointed up the slope. He blended into the white snow; only his blue boots and the skin of his face, his hands, shone darker. He had no hat or gloves, though the coat he wore did have a hood, now hanging down his back, trimmed with thick fur and attached by a zipper. The coat was white nylon, quilted, reaching halfway down his thighs; it looked like something a person, a woman, would wear in a city.

They began to ascend, drifting slightly apart, then closer again. Their shoulders touched when Colville's snowshoes broke through the snow's crust. Within twenty minutes they had crested the slope. Colville looked back at the long indentations in the snow, far below, and then turned to see Jeremy accelerating away, slipping easily down from the ridge, on through a stand of trees with Kilo running alongside him.

He tried to keep up; his pack swayed, his snowshoes clattered and crossed. Jeremy left no real tracks, staying always on top of the snow. Perhaps it was the fact that he traveled so light, carried no pack, but it was also the way he walked: gracefully, his arms swinging in a slow rhythm, his feet lifting eagerly, certain of where they wished to go.

Electric Peak, behind them, slid out of view. Under the trees, the dim light of the afternoon cast few shadows. Colville breathed the cold air in, the hairs in his nose brittle. Wind rattled the branches above, shaking snow loose. It fell silently, disappeared into the whiteness underfoot.

Sometimes Jeremy slipped away, then appeared again, in a farther opening of trees, on a bare expanse of snow; sometimes he seemed to wink in and out of sight from moment to moment, a kind of white mirage with the black shape of Kilo steadily, constantly beside him. They climbed to the next ridgeline, followed it for a while, the cold wind chilling the sweat on Colville's back, under the scarf around his neck, then dropped down into the trees again.

Now Kilo came running back to urge him along, through another rocky gap. Jeremy, waiting there, simply smiled. It was as if they'd met by chance, two lone hikers, as if Jeremy hadn't been exerting himself at all. He stepped to one side, to make room. His beard and mustache framed his white teeth as he reached out his hand, offering a paper cup.

Colville took it, sniffed the white liquid, felt the cold against his fingers. He tasted it. Milk. Next Jeremy handed him a brownie wrapped in cellophane, walnuts visible along its cut edges.

"Listen, Colville," he said. "I need your help. It's that simple. We've been watching you for so long. Those early days with Francine, then Moses. Just the other day I was thinking about your time in Spokane — all those word and number puzzles you used to do, when you were living in that garage. When was the last time you did one of those puzzles, the last time you thought of one?"

Colville stared into the gray sky, uncertain what to say. The wind whistled high in the pines, a rattle of branches, a cold dust of snow shaken loose. He took a bite of the brownie, stale and sweet.

Jeremy swept his fingers up alongside his head as he spoke, as if straightening his hair or clearing it from in front of his eyes, though it stayed in place, combed in waves. To finish the gesture, he stroked his blond beard and mustache as he brought his hand down.

"And you were in that garage when the raccoon found you, and then you found Francine. Your paths, how they fork away from each other and then come together—it's always a pleasure to watch. Francine, she's doing such important work right now, her own preparations."

The wind eased, gusted, spun away through the treetops.

"Sometimes I think I can feel it," Colville said. "Moses. His Light, I mean. The Light Moses had. I think maybe it was thrown to me."

Jeremy sat down on a stump and unlaced his boots. He double-checked the laces, making sure the ends were the same length, knotted them twice, then took a few steps forward and back, checking the fit. When he was satisfied, he looked back up at Colville.

"We should keep moving," he said. "There's still an hour or two of daylight, and people might need our help. We follow this ridge for a time. You lead—I believe I'd welcome a change of pace."

Colville trudged ahead, his breath chuffing out, dispersing. The snow on the ridge was hard, windswept, bare earth peeking through; he considered pausing to take off his snowshoes, but he didn't want to stop, to feel the presence and impatience of Jeremy backed up behind him, where now there was only Kilo's panting. All around, on each side and above, pale clouds slid across each other, higher and lower, their edges sharp. The shadows grew longer; animals flickered at the edges of his vision; crossed branches in bare bushes and fallen trees looked like men, people, figures spying out, gone when he turned his head.

He tried to hike faster, his snowshoes slapping roots and stones, ice. To his right, a steep white slope dropped away, half a mile, to a section of exposed rock, probably a river beneath the ice and snow; to his left, the tree line was about a hundred yards below, mist in the dark, sharp tops of the pines. Was it mist, or were they clouds?

"So—" Colville spoke without turning. "We're up on the Gallatin trail, now?"

There was no answer.

"Past Sportsman Lake?"

Still no answer. At last, he turned. Behind him there was nothing but white snow, whistling wind, the sky turning darker as the sun slid away.

"Jeremy?" he said. "Kilo?" His voice rose as he took two, three steps back in the direction he'd come.

Then he stopped, closed his eyes, shifted the weight of his pack on his shoulders. Should he wait, and for how long? Or should he go ahead?

He turned around again, kept on, farther along the ridge. One foot, then the next, steadily descending, back under the cover of trees. He clapped his gloved hands together in front of him, hummed to himself. His fingers and toes were cold, but he felt confident, certain as he went.

A gunshot. Was it a gunshot? Not far ahead. Or it could have been something else — strange pressure in his ears, a sonic boom, jets hidden high above, or the invisible machines the Messenger wrote about.

Another gunshot, echoing around him, from down below.

And then silence.

Colville picked up his pace, sticks catching and breaking off, kicked free from his snowshoes.

Ten minutes later he came upon it: an elk's head, severed from its body and sitting in the snow. Its black eyes stared; its tongue slightly jutted out between its teeth. It had tipped over slightly, resting on one side of its antlers.

The snow underfoot was red with blood, darker than the shadows, the smell thick in the air. Headless, the carcass hung from a tree limb, half skinned, still dripping. Organs and entrails snaked out, not yet cut free.

Then, beyond the trees, forty feet away and down the slope, he saw movement. Two figures, standing over something. One taller and thinner, and the other talking, shaking his hands in the air. Both men wore camouflage outfits, the taller man in an orange

153

vest. And then the shorter one shouted out: "Is someone there?"

"That's just the elk," the taller man said. "Remember, that's where we hung it. Keep your head, now."

Colville stood still; he considered stepping out of the trees toward the men. They did not look upward, did not call out.

Slowly, very slowly, he eased into movement, skirting the open slope. He stayed low in the underbrush, deeper in the trees, careful that his pack didn't snag on overhanging branches. His heart slowed, his breathing eased. The shadows lengthened and disappeared, joined each other as night fell. Animals called, rustled around him. A tree branch slapped his cheek.

He chewed an icicle, walked farther, followed a streambed covered in snow. A squirrel shot across a branch overhead, leapt to another tree, disappeared. The snow was deeper here, and softer. His snowshoes kicked through to reveal blackened earth; with the smell of ashes in his nose, he kept on, around deadfalls, through the burned-out stretches where fires had run, where new trees now jutted dark through the snow.

He slanted up a ridge, along a cliff, low caves like dark mouths alongside him. A few pale stars now shone between the clouds. It made no sense to worry about Kilo, to try to find Jeremy. That was beyond his power. All he could do was clamber over this ridge, his pack heavy on his back, and start down the other side. Was this Specimen Creek, or was he north of there?

He tripped on a bush, caught himself on a sapling. Holding his breath, he thought he heard something, a mechanical noise, down below. Then it was silent once more, except for his breathing. The wind in the trees, the black sky pressing down close against their branches.

He kept on, descending, along the frozen creek bed. Dark water rushed past, visible through holes in the ice. Again he heard something, and paused. Traffic. He began to see glimpses of a road below, through the trees, a long curved black line against the snow.

The ground grew level after a time, and he emerged from the trees, crossed an empty field. He climbed through a rusted barbed wire fence, up an embankment, then slid down a snowdrift made by plows. He was standing on the narrow shoulder of Highway 191. If he caught a ride north, he'd be in Bozeman; south, in West Yellowstone.

Headlights approached, from the north. A van, its cab alight, slowed; two small, dark-haired girls waved wildly through the side windows, their faces smearing the glass as they slipped past.

Colville hurried, his snowshoes clattering on the blacktop until he reached the other side. He took off his pack and tossed it over the snowdrift, then climbed after it. He began to ascend the next slope, heading deeper into the mountains.

19

THE NEXT MORNING it was still dark when Colville awakened, the air cold against his exposed face. He felt the fabric of the tent close around him, the sleeping bag straining to hold Kilo, as well. It startled Colville that the dog was back, but it did not exactly surprise him.

"Jeremy?" he said, and his voice faded away in the cold darkness around the tent.

Rolling over, he closed his eyes, began his decrees — "I AM the Violet Flame, in Action in me now, I AM the Violet Flame, to Light alone I bow." His voice sped up, a low hum.

Soon, crimson shone through his eyelids. The sun was rising, clearing the ridge. He opened his eyes and the shadows above seemed strange, black lines all around on top of the tent like so many long fingers. Fighting his hands free, unzipping the bag and the tent fly, he crawled out into the freshly fallen snow, stood up in his stocking feet, and turned around.

Sticks, branches, and moss had been piled on his tent, woven into each other, a structure like an upside-down bird's nest, a kind of igloo. White snow and ice glistened on top of it, the sun now shining down. Colville had seen this in his father's survival books; the debris added insulation, kept things warm inside. Jeremy must have done it while Colville slept, before the snow fell; there were no footprints around the structure.

Colville's feet were freezing. He bent down, pulled on another pair of wool socks, found his boots; a few sticks fell from the shelter as he did so, and this rousted Kilo, who crawled out, his body low as if he feared being scratched from above. Once outside, he walked to the remains of last night's fire and turned a slow circle in every direction.

"He's not here," Colville said. "No, don't try to get back in. I know it's cold."

He pulled the tent free, and the structure of sticks and snow leaned but didn't fall; he'd leave this lopsided igloo standing for someone to find, to wonder at. If anyone ever passed through here, wherever this was.

He packed up, then ate breakfast as he walked, hiking up a slope, trying to stay in the sunlight. He held out a handful of dried fish for Kilo, then ate some himself.

They walked all morning, along snowy ridges, through pine forests. West, mostly, as that was the direction that Jeremy had started them in when they first left the shelter. Colville also followed his intuition, tried to sense the energy of a given path; sometimes he followed Kilo, let the dog make the decisions.

When he stopped to rest, he read the passages from *The Art of War* that he'd copied into his notebook: *Some terrain is easily passable, in some you get hung up, some makes for a standoff, some is narrow, some is steep, some is wide open. Appear where they cannot go. Head for where they least expect you. To travel hundreds of miles without fatigue, go over land where there are no people.*

The Teachings said, *Where your thought is, there you are,* and yet all this walking was necessary, a physical demonstration of travel that was not physical. Looking up, Colville checked the cloudless sky for darker patches, bent rays of light. Two hawks hung suspended, inscribing long, smooth circles. One higher, one lower, riding the air currents, their sharp eyes everywhere around him.

◆

Another day passed, a night. They walked along a frozen stream-bed; tall, dried reeds stretched overhead, rain drifted down. Colville could hear Kilo ahead, rustling through the dead reeds, could catch glimpses of his wet, black shape. The yellow stalks shifted the light, made all movement stutter and jerk.

The rain let up just as they reached the cover of trees, thick pines above and tangled ivy below them, a kind of path cutting deeper into the shadows. Kilo paused, shook himself, water spinning away in all directions. Colville tore the plastic bag from his body.

They started up the slope, into a thick forest. Birds called back and forth above; squirrels chittered along low branches. Kilo ran with his nose to the ground, curling away, returning. Colville closed his eyes; he slowed his breath as a wind suddenly rushed at him, the air beating around him. He listened. Something in the grass, smooth along the forest floor, close to him now. When he opened his eyes, it took a moment to see the snake: long and thin, it slid around him, its head down, tongue going, circling, not coming closer. A rattlesnake, its markings pale. Kilo growled; Colville reached down, settled him. Another snake trailed the first, he saw — this one black, a yellow stripe running its length, its head almost touching the tail of the first. Both circled, five feet away, slowly widening their curves and then straightening, heading out under the trees.

Colville followed, one hand on Kilo's neck.

The snakes, still stretched end to end, moved calmly over the roots and stones, around trees and plants, always returning to their course. And then the rattlesnake slipped into a dark round hole in the ground; its body seemed to shorten on itself, its tail going last. The other snake followed, the yellow stripe slipping away, a bright string pulled into the darkness.

Colville's pack caught on a bush, a branch snapping back, a leaf gently slapping him in the face. He held the branch still, his eyes adjusting, focusing close. There, on the leaf's surface, someone had scratched words into the green with a stick or a fingernail: *Hello Friend.* He twisted its stem, broke it loose, folded it away in his pocket. As he did, he glimpsed something above. A flash of white, a movement in the trees. Gone for a moment, there again, too pale and bright to be a leaf—

The white shape seemed to slide along, to climb, high in the branches of the tree. Colville stumbled, his gaze in the trees— there it was again, whatever it was, winking at him, leading him along. He stumbled, looked down, looked up again. Now he saw nothing. Only more branches, the green bushes far below, the soft sound of wind in the pine needles all around him.

A shift, a slight movement, and it all came into focus. Thirty feet above him, fifty feet away. A girl. A girl with long black hair, sitting on a branch, staring straight up through the trees at the sky.

She seemed different from the picture he'd seen—older, thinner—but he knew who she was, recognized her from the poster. She was the girl who had disappeared, the same girl he'd searched for in the foothills of Boise.

Here she was, wherever they were, and he had found her. Barefoot, in jeans and a dark green sweatshirt. Now writing in a notebook; the white page was what he'd seen flashing.

And then the trees swayed. The girl shifted, as if on purpose, testing to see if the air would hold her. She hardly seemed to reach out, to try to catch herself, and she was slipping down through the branches, so slow and smooth, her arms at her sides and her body relaxed, silent as she fell, clattering through the high branches and then out from the low ones, the last ten feet with nothing around her. She landed with a heavy, solid sound. Dust smacked into the air; sticks fell rattling around her.

She was up already, crawling and then running away between the trees, into the bushes and underbrush.

He tried to move quickly, silently, not to lose sight of the way she had gone. Could he see anything ahead, any movement? He wasn't certain.

Kilo led as they crossed a carpet of moss that was every color of green. The ground grew steeper; Colville had to hold on to bushes and tree limbs to keep from falling; he tried not to rustle the branches, to snap any sticks. He leaned his pack against a tree, hardly slowing to set it down as they approached a small clearing.

He crawled forward and lay flat on his stomach, hidden by the bushes. Only twenty feet away, less than that, was the girl.

She was walking in the air, across the air. Five feet off the ground, her arms held out straight from her sides. She stared up into the green trees as she raised one foot, then the other, knees high. It was when she looked down to her feet that she began to sway—slowly at first, then one hand loose and circling around, slapping her leg; she bent at the waist, then hopped down, landing on her feet on the ground. The dark rope she'd been standing on snapped over her head, visible now, swinging and settling, hanging slack where it was stretched between two trees.

And then she turned her head, as if she had heard something.

In a moment a tall, thick man with a black beard stepped into the clearing. He wore a green jacket with black marker scribbled across it, a kind of homemade camouflage. Smiling, he laughed and stepped close to the girl, put his large hand on her shoulder. She said something, reaching up for the rope in the air, and he nodded, took off his jacket, bent to unlace his heavy boots. The girl helped pull them off; she helped unroll his dark socks from his feet.

When the man walked on the rope, it stretched under his weight, only a foot or so above the ground. He was graceful despite his size, smoothly stepping all the way across to the base of one tree, his bare toes on the knot where the rope was tied, then balancing on one foot as he spun around and came back the other way.

Colville could hear his own faint breathing. Kilo, just behind him, hadn't moved at all, as if he understood that they must not be discovered.

Now the man knelt and pulled out a bag, then a backpack, from the bushes. Rummaging inside, he held something — books — in one large hand. He opened one and laid it on a foam mattress in front of the girl, then handed her a pencil. Colville could hear the softness of their voices as they spoke but could not make out the words.

Once the girl began writing in the book — she seemed to be answering a series of questions, or working through equations, or even doing a crossword puzzle — the man crawled around to sit on the mattress also, so their backs leaned against each other. He began to read his own book, holding it open in one hand, close to his face, catching the light. He scratched in his beard with a pencil, underlined a passage, then opened a spiral notebook and wrote something inside.

The girl looked up. She glanced around as if she had heard or smelled something; then, after a moment, she returned to what she'd been writing. Her arms were bare, her sweatshirt sleeves pushed to her elbows. She wore a large watch, a man's watch, on her thin wrist. She turned a page; he wrote something in his notebook.

As the girl read, holding the book open with her toe, she braided her black hair, then pulled out the braid, said something, and the man turned and carefully braided it for her. A French braid, close against her round head. Colville could not hear her, but he could read her lips: *Thank you.*

Squirrels ran past, chasing each other. Gnats hung in the air. Sparrows settled amid the ferns and ivy and sumac, darted away.

And then Colville saw the face. A pale face, in the bushes,

across the clearing from him. Forty feet away, another person, also watching the girl. A man's face. Kilo's tail slapped the ground once, twice, went silent as Colville glanced back. He looked across the clearing again and the face was gone.

The girl said something else, then pointed away into the trees, where the face had been. The man turned quickly, his voice sharp and low; he closed his book, and the girl closed hers as well. Without any more words she leapt up, untied the black rope from between the trees, coiled it. The man rolled the mattress, strapped it to a pack, pulled the other bags together. It took less than five minutes for them to pack it all up, to slip out of the clearing, away through the trees.

Colville crawled backward, struggled to his feet. Kilo followed him to his pack, and then they hurried back up the slope, around the clearing and then into it, across it, trying to figure which way the man and girl had gone. Colville looked at the bushes, uncertain even where he had been hidden. He examined the ground, kneeling, not sure what he was looking for. He would follow them; he would wait until she was alone again, talk to her. But which way had they gone? Between which trees?

"Colville."

Kilo gave a muffled, high-pitched bark at the sound of the voice. Jeremy stepped out of the trees. He had strips of birch bark coiled around his legs and arms, a square of it affixed to his chest so he blended into the stand of trees behind him. It had been him, his face watching from across the clearing—he'd shaved off his beard, and without it he seemed so young, his face more slender and his eyes bigger, bluer. His hair, cropped close to his head, seemed darker.

"This way?" Colville said, trying to walk around him. "Tell me. The girl—"

Jeremy put his hand on Colville's chest, stopping him. "I know," he said. Bending down, he pulled the bark free; it curled upon itself and rolled away, blown by the wind. Now he wore a puffy down jacket, dark purple, and had traded in his moon boots for shiny brown hiking boots with white gaiters.

"Did they go this way?"

"That's the direction they'll go, yes," Jeremy said. "Colville, here, walk with me."

"But what about the girl?"

"She appears to be quite happy, doesn't she?" Jeremy raised his hand to smooth back his hair, lowered it to grasp where his beard had been; he smiled, as if surprised by the skin of his face. "We can observe and we can learn. Her path is her path."

Colville followed Jeremy through a stand of aspens, Kilo running ahead. They walked in silence, Colville trying to figure what to say, glancing back. After ten minutes, they reached a road that stretched down a slope, disappeared around a bend.

"This way," Jeremy said, pointing. "Less than ten miles' walking, to Baker City, but I bet someone will pick you up along the way."

"Her path is living in the woods with that man?" Colville said.

"One thing," Jeremy said, "one thing the girl did, on her path, was to bring you to Francine again. That's the main thing. And the girl's path, there's much to be learned from it. Pay attention. She is a young woman of great Light."

Colville thought he heard a car approaching, but none came. When he looked back, Jeremy was holding out an apple with a blue sticker on it, from a grocery store.

"You've done well," he said. "So far. You'll figure it out as you go, as you have. Just keep paying attention; let your path reveal itself." He pointed down the highway. "You better use the daylight, though."

"And Kilo?"

"He's coming with me." With that, Jeremy squinted up at the sky, nodded once, then turned away. "Kilo!"

Colville could only stand there and watch as Jeremy slipped deeper into the forest; he moved so smoothly, easily, his close-cropped head hardly rising or falling as he walked in and out between the trees, around deadfalls and boulders, Kilo following close behind.

The blouses and dresses on the clothesline were mostly shades of purple, blowing hard in the wind, sideways and up and down. A few were pastel blue or green, none red or black or orange, which were unacceptable colors. They symbolized evil. The Messenger taught that even red roses weren't created by God; they were made out of man's anger. The rage went into the atmosphere and saturated the elements or the beings who made the roses. Roses were meant to be lavender, pink, yellow, or white.

I was trying to help Mrs. Young on this morning. I stretched to reach the line, dropped clothespins in the tall, dry grass. The sun was weaker now, the nights cold. The first snow hadn't fallen yet. All along the yellow hillsides and up toward the canyon other clotheslines waved the same colors, like places where the ground had somehow torn open and blue and green and purple were seeping out.

I could hear heavy machinery, some shelters still being dug, others backfilled. The drills were more frequent now, the preparations more frenzied and anxious.

Down the slope, the Kletter boys were digging in the hillside, a pile of dark dirt next to the hole. Colville went down there to check on their progress and now returned, climbing fast and on all fours, breathing hard when he reached us. He ran a stick along the trailer's metal side, shouted something, threw the stick like a spear up toward the clouds. His white-blond hair blew out sideways, like it was rooted in his brain.

Being close to Mrs. Young made me feel how confused and clumsy and without purpose my own body was. She was talking about the Light she felt, about her baby, about how her body could scarcely contain the energy inside it. She told me about all the preparations she was making, a scrapbook that held pictures of jewels and their alchemical structures along with pictures of cells. The jewels would transmit energy to the baby while Mrs. Young decreed over the book. The diamond would crystallize the baby's will; the sapphire would provide fearlessness, the amethyst forgiveness and transmutation.

I reached for more clothespins, careful as I walked wide around Mrs. Young, afraid to brush against her belly. She said my name, reached out to touch my shoulder. There was a shock, there, a jolt from her body to mine.

20

THE BABY WAS NAKED except for a diaper and the yellow brace-
lets at her wrist and ankle, a white blindfold to protect her eyes.
Her skin glowed. Wells reached out and touched the clear plastic
of the incubator. He leaned close. Her fingers and toes curled, so
tiny, her dark hair growing in every direction. She kicked her leg.
Her mouth twitched, nursed at the air. His daughter. She was five
weeks premature, but healthy — she was only in the incubator as a
precaution. She'd been born in the ambulance, on the way to this
hospital, here in Livingston.

He was alone in the room with her. Two empty, dark incuba-
tors in the corner, a changing table, a cart of diapers and swad-
dling blankets. The lights hummed, shone blue. From the hallway, distant voices, passing footsteps. The baby had come last
night, almost a day ago. Francine had been sleeping, recovering,
during the two hours since Wells had arrived.

"Mr. Davidson?" A nurse stood in the door, behind him.

He turned. "Is she awake?"

"Probably not. It's hard to know with the eye shields on,
though."

"I meant my wife," he said, "whether my wife's awake."

"Would you like me to check?"

"That's all right," he said. "I was about to."

The nurse stepped closer, next to him, looking down at the
baby. "We'll take her out to feed and change her in an hour or so,"
she said. "You can hold her, then."

"Good," he said. "I'll be back."

The white walls confused him; every hallway looked the same. And then, as he walked along a windowed wall, he saw Maya. She waved to him from a waiting room.

"I just left her," she said. "She's still sleeping."

"Am I going the right way? I'll sit with her."

Maya reached out, touched his arm as he turned back toward the hall. "The paramedics from the ambulance last night came by to check on her."

"Are they still here? I'd like to thank them."

"They got called away," she said. "But I talked to them. They told me they got lucky — the baby was so blue it was almost purple. And of course Francine wouldn't sit still. The one guy showed me a bruise on his neck where she kicked him."

Behind Maya the waiting room was empty. Muddy boot prints tracked back and forth across the linoleum floor.

"Also," she said, "your car's here. Francine's car. They said it's fine, the tow-truck people — it was just stuck in the snow."

"Where was it?"

"Somewhere down near Gardiner, I think. She told me she was trying to drive home, back through Yellowstone, but I think the park's been closed for the winter, by the storms."

"Has she said anything?"

"About what?" Maya said.

"I just wish I'd been there, that she'd told me — did she say anything yesterday about what she was doing, or why?"

"She just wanted to come back for a day or two — that's all she said."

"She should have told me," he said.

"Yes," Maya said. "She should have. But what matters is the baby, and that Francine's okay."

"What's the room number, again?"

"One twenty-four. Are you okay?"

Wells went back in the direction he'd come from, turned right, then paused at the door. Slowly he eased it open.

Francine slept, ten feet away, the head of the bed tilted up so she faced him. Her bare arms were outside the blankets, an IV running to one arm, the yellow bracelet on the wrist of the other. The lamp on the bedside table shone faintly. He stepped closer.

She looked tired, and calm. Her hair was spread across the pillow, her eyes closed, her lips faintly twitching. She had done it, and he had been far away, and now he was here. He picked up her hand, held it; she stirred, and for a moment it seemed she might awaken. She settled again. It had been days, only days since he'd seen her. It felt much longer.

"You're here," Francine said, her lips barely moving, her eyes still closed.

"Yes," he said. "Maya called me."

Francine didn't say anything, didn't move. He looked away, at the window, the drawn blinds. He squeezed her hand; she squeezed back.

"I saw the baby," he said. "They say she's doing really well. I haven't held her yet. She's beautiful."

Francine smiled. She opened her eyes halfway, turned her head to look at him.

"When can we go home?" she said.

21

FROM THE BACK SEAT Francine could see past Wells's head as he drove, and through the windshield, through the thick flakes of snow that fell sideways, slanting down. Tall drifts on each shoulder narrowed the highway; semitrailers rushed close, coming from the other direction.

The baby wore a blue stocking cap, her dark hair sticking out one side. Her long eyelashes shifted, and her greenish blue eyes opened. She stared at Francine, those eyes halfway focused, as if she knew something, as if she was not at all surprised to find herself here. And then she closed her eyes and slept again.

They were south of West Yellowstone, now, the Tetons rising on the left. Past Rexburg, heading for Pocatello. Wells tapped a rhythm on the lid of the white plastic bucket in the passenger seat. He still hadn't asked what was in it.

"I can't wait to get home," she said. "It'll be so nice to get her settled, to sleep in our bed, to see old Kilo."

"Three hours, maybe," he said. "A little longer if we stop or the weather gets worse. I wish we could have gone down 89. Past where you grew up and everything. I'd have liked to see that."

"There's not much to see anymore," she said. "And this road is open. This is the way I drove, coming up the other night."

"Kilo went missing," Wells said. "He's out, somewhere. Probably looking for you."

"He didn't find me."

"Once you're home, he'll come back." Wells checked the rear-view mirror. "Is she sleeping?"

"I think so."

Francine gazed out at the pines ticking past, her head against the window. She closed her eyes. Highway 89 was the route she'd wanted to take, two days ago, when she'd left the hot springs. She'd felt the pull toward the Heart; she'd wanted to drive close, to see it, for the baby inside her to feel it. And she'd tried—she'd driven down Paradise Valley, powdery snow drifting sideways across the highway, toward Gardiner. She turned off at Corwin Springs, re-membering all the times with her family in the station wagon, safe, the cars of others in the Activity in front of and behind them. It felt so close to the same, her anticipation rising—she crossed the rickety bridge, the half-frozen river rushing below; she drove past the blue and purple buildings, past King Arthur's Court and up into the narrow canyon that led to the Heart. The air thick-ened around her, the pull stronger, the treetops leaning in above the road. But the snow grew too deep before she could get as close as she wanted, and the car slid sideways into a ditch when she tried to turn around. It was then that her water broke, that the contractions started. She was stranded for almost an hour be-fore the two men—one in a truck, one on a snowmobile—found her. They called the ambulance and waited with her until it came. The men were from the Activity, but she didn't know them. They didn't even know anyone she knew.

"Are you asleep?" Wells said.

"No," she said. "Not yet."

"While you were gone—" He glanced back in the rearview mir-ror, his sweet, worried eyes, then through the windshield again. "Why did you go like that?"

"I don't know," she said. "I just did it."

"You should have told me."

"I'm sorry."

"It felt," he said. "It felt like you were trying to get away."

"That's not it," she said. "That's not right."

"I would've understood," he said. "Or tried to. I think I understand better, now."

Outside, the snow came down thicker, faster. He switched on the wipers, switched them off.

"Maybe I shouldn't have," he said. "Maybe you'll be angry, but I read about it — everything you wrote, about when you were growing up."

Draft horses stood out in a field, snow on their broad backs. Tall fences against the elk surrounded haystacks. Farther away, a small herd of antelope shifted at the sound of the car, then leapt fluidly over a wheeled irrigation line that had been left out for the winter.

"Are you warm enough, back there?"

"Yes."

"It really made me miss you," he said. "Reading it did. Are you mad?"

"I didn't write it for you."

"You were gone. I didn't know — "

"It's fine," she said. "Maybe it's better, I think it is — I'm glad you read it. But I wrote it for myself." Shifting in her seat, she looked at the sleeping baby's smooth face, adjusted the blankets. "I wrote it for her, too. So she could understand."

Francine watched as Wells reached out, turned up the heat, the defrost. Black stripes, tire tracks marked the white highway, left by vehicles she couldn't see, fading to white as the snow fell.

"Did you find it?" he said.

"Find what?"

"The reason you went there," he said. "Are you glad you did it?"

"I should have told you," she said.

"But you had to go."

"Yes," she said. "And I feel better, I feel better to be talking about it, for us to be talking."

"It all sounded so happy, back then," he said.

"It was."

"I was thinking," he said, "before, when you were asleep, how this driving was kind of like your family, when you were a girl, how maybe we — our family — were driving over the same roads, all these years later."

"Yes," she said.

"Only you had two girls," he said. "And that picture on the dashboard, that angel."

"Archangel Michael," she said. "Yes. It was only a piece of paper, but it looked like stained glass. And we decreed as we went."

"How did that sound?"

"It doesn't matter."

"It does," he said. "I want to hear it."

Leaning forward, she gathered all her hair together in one hand, pulled it back from her face, tucked it behind her shoulder. Then she closed her eyes and began:

> *"Lord Michael before, Lord Michael behind,*
> *Lord Michael to the right, Lord Michael to the left,*
> *Lord Michael above, Lord Michael below,*
> *Lord Michael, Lord Michael, wherever I go!*
> *I AM his Love protecting here!*
> *I AM his Love protecting here!*
> *I AM his Love protecting here!"*

Silence. The snow slanted down; the wind blew it loose from the green trees along the highway. The baby's eyes jerked open; Francine felt the vibrations of her voice, the words settling around them.

"Thank you," Wells said.

"Feel safer, now?" she said.

"In a way, I think I do."

"It woke up this little girl, in any case."

The baby began to cry; her face turned impossibly red, her little hands suddenly loose and flailing.

"Can you pull over, so she can nurse?"

Wells found a turnout, eased over the frozen crust of tire tracks; the car slid a little, then stopped, settled. Francine unbuckled her seat belt, unzipped her coat, unbuttoned her blouse. The baby began to quiet as soon as she was lifted; she weighed so little, her gums showing, her mouth sucking at the air and then latching on, her arms pushing, her hands trying to hold.

It was silent again. Snow drifted down, settling on the hood of the car, slowly piling up on the windshield wipers. Francine watched the baby's jaw flex, and the pale blue veins that forked along her skull, disappearing under her knit cap. She'd come from far away and grown inside her and now here she was, outside. The blanket around her tiny body rose and fell, her breathing.

"You're crying," Wells said, turning in his seat, watching.

"It's just that I'm so happy," she said. "It's so hard to believe that we get to keep her, we get to have this little person."

"Have you thought of any names?"

"Not yet," she said. "We're still getting to know her. Soon."

It was a little sad to look back at our trailer, unlit and abandoned, knowing we might never live there again. I slipped on the ice, held my mom's hand. No one was yelling yet, or hurrying. There was a kind of purpose, a quiet purpose guiding us along. We didn't talk. Somewhere a dog was barking, somewhere I couldn't see.

People joined us, above and below, people forked away to other shelters. Flashlights and camping lanterns shone against the darkness. There was hardly any sound at all. Far below on the highway an endless line of cars crept south, some turning off at Glastonbury, most keeping on toward Corwin Springs. Even miles away, through the snow, I could see all the things piled atop the vehicles, all the last-minute supplies and belongings that couldn't be left behind.

Twenty or so people gathered near the tunnel that led to the shelter, the ground there all scraped free of snow. More lanterns were set up and two of the workmen were telling people how much they could carry in. To one side, duffel bags and suitcases and trash bags were piled up. People dug through them, sorting, deciding. Other people who didn't have a space in the shelter were crying, pleading, trying to talk their way in. They had no place to go, and now the time had come. March 15, 1990.

The men knew us; they waved us through the door and we hurried down the steep wooden stairs with the warmer air rising around us, the darkness giving way to lights as we reached the bottom, where we kicked off our boots into a pile of boots and shoes. Everyone had to wear slippers inside, to keep out the dirt and dust. We had to keep everything as clean as we could, to keep the ventilators from working too hard.

The second door was also metal, and would close the shelter off from the entryway. We went through it, into the hallway, which was crowded with people I knew and people I didn't know. Everyone just buzzed; it was all finally happening.

We forced our way past, out for a moment into a wider space of the eating area and the kitchen, people busy sorting pots and pans, counting chairs. They were talking about pancakes in the morning, and I started to wonder how we would know what time of day it was if we couldn't see the sky, if all the clocks and watches ran down. I decided it might not matter.

Maya had slipped ahead, people between us. She was already moving farther down the curved hallway, beyond our door. My mother called after her, then told me to wait in our room.

I walked down the hallway and opened the door. Number 7. I stepped inside and closed the door. Everything was quieter, everything in its place. I climbed up into my bunk, which I'd climbed into so many times before this one night that mattered. Here was the quilt that smelled like my mom, since she had made it, and the sweet chemical smell of the new foam rubber mattress, and the smell of the wood that had been bent to cover all the walls. I rolled over, onto my back. Two knots in the wood just above me stared down like eyes. I looked at them and knew they'd become so familiar to me in the days and nights to come.

I listened for my mom and Maya, for their voices in the shouting, and couldn't be certain. Down below, our room was so neatly packed, all finished now. All the clothes and shoes of my future body, all the books and encyclopedias and dictionaries, all the first aid and wilderness guides. So many things packed up in plastic trash cans with their locking lids, the big Tupperware containers that fit beneath the bed, in the spaces under the floorboards;

it all reminded me of playing with Colville in the shed outside our trailer, where our parents were gathering all their canning and everything. We'd rearrange the boxes full of food so it was a kind of fort, a shelter that would protect us and that we could eat.

Colville wasn't so far away, just down the highway; still, he could be on the other side of the world, considering how far apart we were at that moment, how impossible to reach him. We might not see each other until we were teenagers. Would we still be friends? What would we talk about? I imagined how it would be if he burrowed a tunnel to me, between the shelters. I'd hear a scratching through the wall and then he would come through, dirt in his hair, his body older, a man's body, and still my friend. Was Colville asleep right now? Was he thinking of me?

I couldn't sleep. I counted the containers, waiting. All this my parents had done for us, and they knew what they were doing, and I was not afraid because I knew they would be with me, underground in the shelter, no matter how long it took. I found this reassuring, and also it made me think of my grandparents, my parents' parents, who were far away and on the outside. I hadn't seen them very often, and now we might never see them again. There was a photograph of my mom's parents, on a bookshelf. They stood in front of a red car and my grandpa had a small mustache, his arm around my grandma's shoulder.

The door beneath my bed suddenly swung open and I turned over and saw the top of Maya's head, her crooked part, then my mom's. Maya took two steps up a ladder and fell face-down onto her cot. She lay still. My mom turned to check, to see where I was; she didn't smile.

Maya snuffled, turned her face sideways where I could see it, red and teary. Her friend Courtney had run away; she'd gone with people who weren't in the Activity, people she knew somehow. Maya told me that, then stopped talking. She sobbed every now and then, shifted her body, and I heard her whispering Reverse the Tides decrees, and then she slowed down and finally fell asleep. I watched her the whole time, thinking how sad it was that she had planned to have her friend along with her, underground, and now would not. Then I realized that Maya was not crying because of that, or not only because of that; it was more that Courtney didn't believe and so she would be exposed, out in the open most likely when the blast came. That meant she would really be gone.

I rolled onto my back again and stared at the knothole eyes. I felt bad for Maya, losing her friend and not knowing what had happened. At the same time, it meant that she would have more time for me, and that made me happy, since I didn't have many friends in the shelter. I'd expected that Colville would be there, three doors away, and he wasn't; instead he was down at the ranch, in the big shelter. I imagined how happy he had to be, underground, to finally have the waiting over, to find out what was going to happen.

We hadn't heard about Mrs. Young's baby, so maybe it hadn't been born yet and would be born underground and wouldn't even see the sky until he wasn't even a baby anymore. He would be a boy, a special boy like the Messenger had said. Would his eyes work, out in the daylight? Would his pale skin burn too easily? Would he always want to live underground? Would he wear sunglasses, even inside?

I couldn't sleep. A man in the hallway was asking something about the ventilation system. Someone answered him, voices trailing away. Someone else said something about an electrical line and North Glastonbury; a woman shouted about a telephone tree; beneath and beyond the close voices there was the rhythm of decrees, all through the shelter.

We did have pancakes in the morning, a happy breakfast underground before we surfaced again, into the blue sky, the bright clear day. Some people celebrated because we had turned away the darkness for a time — that's what the Messenger told us. Prophecy is not written in stone, she said, and already she was drifting away, her soul leaving her body. Some people blamed her, and some kept on as if nothing had changed, even if the nature of this world is change. Some people believed that the world had ended, that the bombs had come, and that we were left to live in a kind of copy that was so close to what had been. Others were confused, and some left the Activity. Some, like Colville's family, drifted away, splintered off to start other Activities, like the Temple of the Presence, down in Tucson. Some people were angry, or felt tricked. Many had debts from the preparations, the construction, all the years of food and supplies they'd bought. The world remained; the banks and governments had not disappeared. All the problems that had been left aboveground were still there, still here, waiting.

Lying there that night, in my bunk above the doorway, what I mostly felt was happy. I had chosen the family I was born into, and we were here for a reason. We had been warned, and we had prepared ourselves. We had gathered the Light and we would continue, even in the years underground, even after that. I stared up at the two knothole eyes and imagined the concrete behind the wood, and then all the dirt and earth piled on top of that. If I dug upward forty feet I'd be out in the cold again, where the snow was probably still falling and that dog I'd heard was still barking, lonely, wandering around and through the quiet and lonely houses, searching. Perhaps with his ears he could hear the missiles long before they arrived, as he ate forgotten food from countertops, as he shook snow from his fur and whined quietly to himself. A black dog, racing across the snow. He scratched, he whined and sniffed at the metal doors of one shelter, then ran toward the next, barking and barking, and no one could hear him.

22

COLVILLE CHECKED BEHIND HIMSELF; even now, he kept expecting Kilo to be there, or to appear, to draw attention or give
him away. And yet the dog was not here. He'd been taken somewhere else by Jeremy. Colville was on his own.

In the darkness, he leaned against the fence, its splintery wood
against his lips, only his eyes peeking over the top, across the back
yard, at the darkened house. It was after ten, still before midnight. A foot of snow capped the picnic table.

He'd left his gloves behind in the pack; with his hands in his
pockets, it was difficult to balance on the bucket he'd found. The
ground beneath the bucket was all ice, and icicles hung in the
sagebrush on the hillside that stretched up behind him, that he
had descended not long before.

Wells, that was the husband's name, and when a light suddenly
shone in a window it was Wells standing there, just staring for
a moment, rubbing at one eye. He was in the kitchen — Colville
remembered the layout of the house, from the one time he'd been
inside it; he'd drawn a diagram of it in his notebook. Close, maybe
forty feet away, but with the light on, Wells could only see his own
reflection. Now he looked down and turned on a faucet, began to
wash dishes.

Colville's legs ached from balancing. He waited and watched,
the rough fence against his face. This day had started so long
ago — the same day that he'd found the girl, that he'd walked out
of the mountains and found that he was in Oregon. He'd caught

185

the bus in Baker City and a few hours later got off in Boise. And now here he was, watching Wells, who was squinting through the other window, over the driveway, out the side of the house. Wells switched off the kitchen light, so he could see out, and then Colville could follow his gaze, upward, two houses over, to the lost girl's house, where an upstairs window was alight in an empty room.

Were cats fighting, somewhere? There was a crying. A bird? Colville smelled wood smoke on the cold air. Headlights came down the street, visible in the gaps between the houses, then tailed away. Pulling a hand from his pocket, he steadied himself, listened. He heard only distant traffic.

Wells switched the kitchen light back on and another window went alight at the same moment. The bathroom, the narrow window of thick, textured glass: Colville could see only the silhouette, but he knew the color of Francine's hair, moving back and forth, her body growing smaller as she turned away. At the sight of her he inhaled the sharp, icy air; he tried to exhale slowly, in pieces, letting just a little steam escape at a time. The bathroom window went dark.

Colville glanced at the window of the other house. A yellow rectangle, high in the air, light spilling out across the roof of a garage.

Now, in the kitchen window, Francine appeared, wearing a blue robe, carrying something in her arms. Suddenly Colville felt as if a large, warm hand pressed flat across his chest, a deep vibration over his heart; all of his fingertips and toes felt grasped at once, pulled straight out and let go. His vision clouded white, returned just as the baby's red face, tiny, showed for a moment between the folds of Francine's robe. He could hear the squalling, the gasps between the wails.

Wells turned from the sink, held out his arms, but Francine smiled and shook her head, swayed her body side to side. She held the baby close as it quieted, as it turned its face away from where Colville could see. Climbing down, he picked up the bucket and carried it along the fence line, put it back where he'd found it. It was better to move while Francine and Wells were in a lighted room, where it would be more difficult to see his dark shape scurrying against the white slope.

He climbed, the cold growing sharper, tighter around him. When he reached the first line of brush, he bent down behind it and looked back. The kitchen light still shone, though he could see no shapes, no shadows inside it. The light in the other house was out, however, that whole house dark, the white snow a moat around it, glowing against the night. Looking down from this height, Colville expected to see the dark circle of the trampoline.

He thought of the girl, the lost girl's sister. He remembered her. He remembered that the time he spoke to her, they had been right at the same place where he stood now. This hollow in the thick brush, the small overhang where he'd left his books, his tape recorder, the cassette tapes of the Messenger's decrees. Earlier — an hour ago? — he'd returned to this place, stashed his frame pack before descending to Francine's house; now he pulled the pack from under the overhang, across the icy ground. Taking out his headlamp, he shone a beam back as far as he could. A few tangled strands of tape reflected back, plastic shards of broken cassettes. The tape recorder was no longer here. The books, probably burned into the ashes that blackened the rocks to one side.

Soon he approached a house under construction, perched on top of the ridge. Yellow plastic tape circled it, signs warned against trespassing. Shivering, he felt someone watching, eyes on him, then waited until the feeling passed. He walked around a bulldozer, its metal treads frozen in glassy puddles, and squinted at the house's new windows, all closed. A sheet of plywood had been attached across the front door, another NO TRESPASSING sign nailed to its center.

Circling the house, he peered down into the cement window wells. He lifted a metal grate, slid it away, dropped his pack to the gravel below, then lowered himself down. This window was locked. When he kicked it in, the glass shattered on the floor inside. He eased himself carefully over the sill, then reached back for his pack, fished out his headlamp. He held it in his hand, shielding it; he didn't want it to flash up the stairs, out a window, to be seen by someone below.

The metal ductwork shone overhead, but there was no furnace, not yet. The stairs that stretched up were rough, temporary, and the rest of the house, as he moved through it, seemed similarly unfinished. In some rooms, drywall had been hung, and in others the walls were only exposed studs, water pipes snaking here and there, the white zigzags of electrical wire strung from outlet to outlet. The air hung cold and still, thick with the smell of sawdust. The plywood subflooring echoed slightly beneath his boots. The kitchen cabinets had been installed, yet had no doors; the tile work in the bathroom was half finished. A toilet rested on its side in the hall.

There were signs of work, of workers — loose nails glinted along the floor, and a carpenter's belt was coiled in one corner, a 7-Eleven coffee cup on a windowsill — but it felt to Colville that it had been a while, that the money had run out or winter had slowed things.

He paused, held himself perfectly still, listened for one minute, two. Nothing.

The picture window in the front room overlooked the city, lights glowing in a sleepy grid. Closer, down the long slope, all the windows of Francine's house were now dark. Snow was beginning to fall. The girl's house, too, was all in shadow. Had he walked close by the lost girl and the man, when they'd been hiding up in these hills? He had not known, not seen or heard them. Perhaps he had missed them by days, or only hours, arrived in Boise moments too late. Finding her then hadn't been part of his path. If he had found the girl, back then, would he have returned to the shelter, or met Jeremy? Would he be freezing right now in this half-built house, uncertain what he was supposed to do next?

Dragging two sawhorses across the room, he stretched a blue tarp across them, making a kind of tent. He folded the edges around, weighed them down, then opened a roll of pink insulation, tore it into long pieces, and put it on top of the tarp. Next, he slid two more strips under the tarp, the pink side down, brown paper up. He kicked off his boots, unrolled his sleeping bag, climbed inside. The tarp sagged down, a slight pressure on him from above. He zipped the bag tightly against his chin, only his face exposed. He closed his eyes and slept.

◆

A noise, somewhere in the house. Someone searching through the rooms, then a scratching overhead. Not exactly footsteps. Colville squinted out, along the floor. Were the sounds coming closer? He had to pick his moment, then crawl out, take his boots and pack, slip quietly down the stairs, into the window well. Had there been a ladder, in that space, a way to climb out? Or would he be trapped there, waiting to be discovered? The sound of breathing came closer.

And then, just as he had his arms free, as he began to reach for his boots, the black dog came skittering through a doorway at him, licking his face, whining. Colville scratched Kilo's neck, slapped the skin of his belly as he rolled over.

"Good morning," Jeremy said, standing there. He wore the white quilted parka again, the blue moon boots on his feet. "Hot water," he said, holding out the 7-Eleven cup that Colville had seen last night. "I remembered how you used to drink that some mornings. Here's a couple doughnuts, as well. Aren't you surprised to see me?"

"I don't know."

"You were having such a good time, I know, making decisions on your own, all the responsibility. You were doing quite well."

Jeremy stepped to one side, reached out to touch the sawhorse structure, the tent of tarps and insulation. "But I realized that you very well might need Kilo here after all."

The dog, sitting close against Jeremy's legs, looked up at the sound of his name. Colville felt the heat of the water through the cup in his hand.

"Did you bring the girl?" he said.

Jeremy looked out the window, at the pale sky. Colville just watched, sipped at the hot water, waited.

"I thought I made it clear that she can't come back here," Jeremy said. "Not like that. I believe I suggested, at the very least, that she was following her own path. I asked you to learn from her, to pay attention." He clapped his hands, opened them to reveal a roll of bills, held them out to Colville.

"I'll be all right."

"Take it, just in case you need it. You can never be certain what will happen — "

"Yes," Colville said, folding the money away. "I know that." His boots were cold, stiff. He laced them tightly, rolled up his sleeping bag, then stuffed it into his orange pack. Crouching there, he tried to decide whether to take down his makeshift tent, whether or not it mattered.

"As you know," Jeremy said, "it's up to you. I have every confidence, of course — no one else could do what you will, no one else would even know where to start. And you'll do it calmly, you know, as if it's already been done — "

As he spoke, Jeremy gave a kind of half-wave, stepping through a doorway, wandering into another room as if trying to understand the house's layout. His voice continued, difficult to hear, and then there was only silence. Colville waited. Kilo followed through the same doorway, then returned, sniffing the floor.

Colville stood after a moment, leaving the tent as it was. Slowly he walked around the dim, half-built house, from room to room. Jeremy was gone. It made no sense to call his name.

In the small room next to the kitchen, on the other side of the house, a glass door opened onto a wooden deck. Colville unlocked the door, slid it open, and stepped through; he waited for Kilo to follow before sliding it closed again. The houses on either side were built farther down the slope, their windows beyond where he could see. That meant no one looking out could see him as he stepped into the open.

In the new snow around the house, he could reconstruct the comings and goings of the night before. The tracks of two rabbits, then a coyote, not long after, slowing and then jogging away, up the ridge. Birds had settled, flown off again. Kilo's prints approached the front door — the plywood still nailed tight there — then stopped at once, as if he'd been lifted into the air. Jeremy had left no footprints that Colville could see.

"Come on, boy," he said, and Kilo ran back, stayed close alongside him. The dog had to recognize where they were; so close to Francine's, to his old home. They did not walk in that direction, but over the other side of the ridge, down to a paved road that curved around, that would lead them back to the city. Colville's skin itched, probably from the pink insulation, maybe even from yesterday's haircut. The blacktop was icy, slushy; they stayed on the shoulder, though no traffic came past. This morning, he suddenly realized, Jeremy had looked the same as always — his blond hair smoothly swept back, his thick beard combed into a point. As if it had all grown back overnight.

23

COLVILLE TRIED TO IMAGINE everything that could go wrong and how to make it right. He'd been preparing his whole life, especially these last few weeks, since the raccoon had found him in Spokane.

He'd spent most of the day planning and preparing, buying the things he'd need. He did his decrees and meditated in his motel room; he went over and over the passages he'd copied into his notebook: *Observe a person's or animal's routine, find the weak point in that routine, and then enter the weak point and move with it, thus becoming invisible to everyone. This dead space exists in both nature and the city. Even those people walking alone at night, fearful of attack or robbery, frightened and hypervigilant, still have countless dead spaces in which one can operate. Even those who stalk have this dead space.*

Now energy radiated out, all around as he walked through the dark neighborhoods, returning to Francine's house. Kilo pranced down the icy sidewalk, running ahead and returning with his snout in the air. He seemed to recognize where they were.

Colville's frame pack was light, empty of almost all the things left back in the motel room. He swung the pack around, set it down in the vacant lot at the end of the block, in the dark shadows of the fence, then pulled off his black nylon poncho so he was wearing the white hooded sweatshirt he'd bought earlier; with the white sweatpants, he would be more difficult to see against the snow.

The sweatshirt and pants were silent as he crept along the fence behind the houses. Kilo stayed close; he didn't need a leash, he could sense by the way Colville was moving — arms out for balance, lifting his knees high and setting only the balls of his feet gently down — that this was no time to stray.

Colville reached to touch Kilo's neck, and the dog sat down, waiting, watching as Colville pulled himself upward, peeked over. Only one light was on, deep in the house, probably in the living room.

It took a moment to find the loosened boards in the fence where Colville had taken Kilo, but when he did he worked them free from the ice and pried them out again. Just enough so that, on his hands and knees, twisting sideways with a nail snagging his sweatpants, his bare hip sliding, cold, he could pull himself through, into the back yard. He remained on his stomach, spread out on the white snow. No sounds, no voices, no lights turning on. Next he held the boards back and took Kilo by the scruff of the neck, helped him through. He held the black dog close, hugged him tight, whispered in his ear: "Thanks, boy. You're home again. Remember what to do."

Kilo whined once as Colville dragged himself, then crawled away, past the picnic table, standing very slowly to open the gate that led to the driveway. Once there, he crept around to the other side of Francine's car, knelt down, and waited. A light on the garage, attached to a motion sensor, switched on. Brightness, black shadows suddenly everywhere. After a moment the light switched off again. Silence.

And then Kilo began barking. Tentatively at first, and then, as lights came on in the house, more loudly. Colville could hear him running in circles, tearing around the yard as he barked, his claws scratching the wood of the fence as he reared up on his hind legs, as he changed direction.

The door opened at the side of the house, twenty feet from Colville.

"Kilo?" Francine said. "What?"

Colville squinted through the window, across the inside of the car and out the windshield. It was impossible to see her clearly, only the shape, the blue of her robe and then a blur of red as Wells came out behind her.

"Is it really him?"

They rushed down the stairs, so close to Colville, then opened the gate to the back yard. Kilo was still barking, still running, unable to calm down. When the wooden gate swung shut, Colville could no longer see Francine and Wells. That meant that they could no longer see him. Now was his moment.

Moving quickly across the narrow space, up the few stairs, Colville opened the door, slipped into the kitchen. Staying low, out of sight in the windows, the house now all alight, he crawled past the table, past the sink full of dirty dishes, the refrigerator with a card that said "Congratulations on Your Baby Daughter!" attached by a magnet shaped like the letter *F*. He stood up when he was in the hallway, pausing once to listen — Kilo still barking, the voices still outside — and he opened the door slowly, squinted into the bathroom. No. Backing up, he opened the door he'd passed. The sound of wind rose up, startling him; it came from a small round machine on the floor, plugged into the wall beneath a growing green nightlight. His eyes slowly adjusted. He stepped over the cord, around a laundry basket, to the crib.

The baby's eyes were closed. She slept. Colville lifted one blanket and saw that she was swaddled in another, wrapped tightly. She wore a stocking cap, striped, with a tassel. Only her small face was exposed.

He hesitated. The air buzzed and shuffled; the sound of the wind was everywhere; it covered any sound he might make, would muffle the baby if she cried, but it also deafened him to what has happening outside. He'd have no warning if Francine and Wells began to return.

The baby pursed her lips, whimpered slightly as he lifted

her — she was lighter than he expected — but she did not awaken. On the way out of the room, he took a handful of clothes from the laundry basket, another blanket from the shelf beneath the changing table.

A sound, the kitchen door opening. He stepped sideways from the hallway into the living room, past a baby swing and a stack of cardboard boxes. He breathed silently. He tried to hold himself invisible, to believe it as he heard Kilo clatter into the kitchen — claws on the linoleum, tail slapping the cabinets, the refrigerator.

"Settle him down," Francine said. "Keep him quiet."

"Here you are," Wells was saying, the pitch of his voice rising. "We didn't get rid of your bowls. No, we didn't. We wouldn't do that, Kilo."

As Colville stood there in the living room, holding the baby, Francine came down the hallway. Her lips were moving but she was not saying anything aloud; her hair was pulled loosely back, a strand hanging in front of her face. She looked tired and strong and she did not notice him, standing so close.

Once she was past, Colville glanced at the baby in his arms. Her eyes were open, gazing up at him as if she recognized and had been expecting him. He felt her breathing, her heartbeat, the vibrations so calm in their rhythm together. Still she made no sound.

He took two steps and carefully turned the knob of the front door. The hinges squeaked only slightly as he eased it open. The storm door, next, the laundry held in his armpit and the baby cradled as he carefully stepped off the porch. Across the icy walk they went. Up the street, under the bare branches of the trees.

His pack leaned against the fence where he'd left it, and he opened its flap with his free hand, pushed the laundry into a side pocket. The main compartment was lined with his down sleeping bag, open, soft, and warm. In the faint light he could see that the baby's eyes were closed again. Her mouth seemed to curl in a faint smile. Gently, he eased her into the pack, then wrapped the sleeping bag around, pulled down the flap. Next he took out his black poncho, pulled it on, and carefully lifted the pack to his shoulders.

Colville listened; he heard nothing. No voices, no sirens. He began to walk through the dark streets, back toward the motel. Perhaps Francine had been going to check on the baby, or perhaps she had gone to the bathroom, or back to her bedroom to sleep. She had not seen him, and she had been so close.

He heard a car horn, distant traffic. No sirens, no shouting voices. A television glowed blue through a curtained window. A cat slipped quietly past, leaping a stretch of ice. Colville listened to the baby's soft, sweet breathing as she slept in the pack, her mouth so close to his ear.

24

THE BABY SLEPT. Colville had changed her diaper twice, careful to memorize the folds of the blanket that swaddled her. When she was awake, she kicked her legs, grabbed hold of his fingers; he had worried about her crying, that it would draw attention, but she'd hardly made a sound.

She slept on the queen bed farther from the door of the motel room, closer to the kitchenette. He rested next to her, *Dr. Spock's Baby and Child Care* open on his chest. The bottles and nipples he'd boiled stood lined on the kitchenette counter. Next to them, the tins of formula, the glass jars of baby food. Squash, green beans, bananas, all pureed.

The room was dim, the only light from the digital clock — 2:45 — and the sliver from the bathroom, that door ajar. Colville believed that he could feel it, the purity of energy that Jeremy mentioned, the clear vibrations that spun out from the baby. She shifted a little. Her chest rose and fell: she breathed.

He should sleep also, but he could not sleep. There was too much he didn't know, too much he had to figure out. The information about how to care for her physically — that he could learn, he could read about. He could watch her closely and react. It wouldn't be easy, he didn't want it to be easy, but he knew he could do it. Otherwise why would he have been led on this path, entrusted with her? What he needed to know was how to protect a baby's Light, how to prepare her. He remembered how it had been with Moses — one rule was that no one was allowed to touch the top of the baby's head; another was that no one outside the family was allowed to hold the baby for the first six months. These were the kind of Teachings he needed, and he had given Francine all the books that contained them.

Then, a pale band of light. Along the dark, wood-paneled wall, three feet from the bed. Colville thought of headlights, checked the curtains — they were closed; it was dark at the window.

Careful not to wake the baby, he sat up and swung his legs around, put his bare feet on the floor between the two beds. He stood and walked around to the baby's side of the bed, closer to the wall. As he turned, he felt and saw the pale light on his dark T-shirt, flickering across his chest. He checked the dark window again.

The light was coming from the baby. She still slept, but the skin of her face, turned toward the wall, cast an even glow. He felt every hair on his head tighten, pulse. He pulled his hand out of the light, rubbed it against his shirt.

"Colville," a voice said.

He froze, glanced toward the door, then crept along the carpet, moving on his toes, on his fingertips. He checked the dead bolt, the chain. Everything was locked. Pressing his ear to the door, he heard nothing. Had someone really said his name? He still did not stand up; he stayed low as he moved past the window, as if there were a gap in the curtains. There wasn't.

Once he reached the bathroom, he pushed the door gently open, leaned in, looked into the bathtub. Nothing, no one.

"Baby food?" the voice said, everywhere in the room at once. "I can't even roll over yet and you expect me to eat baby food?"

Colville stepped back into the room. The dark shape in the mirror, his own body, startled him. The back of his hand brushed the television's dark screen and it crackled, a sudden shock.

"I'm surprised you hesitate to see," the voice said, "you who believed your childhood friend came back to call on you in the form of a badger."

Colville stepped into the space between the two beds, closer to the baby.

"Don't look at me while I'm talking," she said. "Not my face. Don't look at my face."

Colville sat on the other bed, his eyes closed. He tried to slow his breathing, his heart.

"Better," she said, after a moment.

"It was a raccoon," he said. "You know that, you have to know that."

"A raccoon? Was it? You're probably right." The baby made a noise like a laugh, an intake of breath that sounded like tearing paper.

"You have to tell me," he said. "I know I'm not supposed to touch the top of your head. I don't even know if I'm supposed to even hold you."

"There are exceptions," she said. "How am I going to move anywhere if you don't hold me?"

Her voice was low, breathy, somewhere between a man's voice and a woman's voice. It didn't so much echo in the room as appear suddenly in his ears, and as she spoke her words came more slowly, more softly, as if she were drifting off to sleep. Colville sat in silence; carefully, he opened his eyes. The baby still lay there, swaddled. He could not tell if her eyes were open, as her face was tilted toward the wall.

"Who are you?" he said.

"Who have I been, or who will I become?"

Without warning the baby let out a little cry, a rising squall. The surface of the blanket moved as she tried to get her arms free.

"What should I do?" he said.

"I have to sleep," she said. "Don't look at me while I'm talking. Remember that. My diaper's wet, too. Change it, please, so I can sleep. I get tired so fast with this talking, it's ridiculous."

He stood, his legs unsteady beneath him. Reaching into the packet for a new diaper — they were a little large, but his guess had not been far off—he began to unfold the blanket that swaddled the baby. He was still anxious about looking at her, afraid she might begin speaking again; this made the operation impossible. She began to cry as he fumbled, and he hurried, trying to stop the sound. Her lips curled back over her gums, her toothless mouth. She turned her head to watch what he was doing, and her dark eyes didn't seem to quite focus on him. They drifted, cloudy, they rolled, and they closed again as he snapped the sleep suit back on, as he wrapped the blanket tightly around her.

He laid her down, stretched himself alongside her, as they had been before. There was only the slight sound of her breathing. It sped up, it slowed down. She sighed in her sleep. The pale light still shone from her, a band of it glowing along the paneling of the wall.

Colville tried to settle his body, his emotions inside it, and also his thoughts. This baby he'd been given, she was an honor and a responsibility at once. She seemed to know so much, and yet there would be so many things that she couldn't do, so many things that could happen to her that she wouldn't be able to prevent. In his notebook he'd copied a passage that the Messenger had written, how at her birth and in her early years she had been aware of the realms of Light from which she'd descended, had been able to recall her previous embodiments, but that this awareness faded as the soft spot at the crown of her head closed over and as the adults around her discouraged such talk, calling it fantasy. With this baby, he would encourage her to remember, to stay in contact with the Light so she could bring it more fully into the world. This he would do.

He thought of the Messenger, her body still alive, walking and talking in Bozeman, and her soul adrift and traveling, perhaps finding a home, a return in this baby sleeping next to him. He looked down at her, tucked against his ribs, her skin so smooth and faintly glowing. The soul moved from one to the next, necessary shelters and vehicles on its path.

"Colville? Are you awake?"

Had he slept? The clock now read 6:20.

"I'm awake," he said.

"You're doing the best you can, I know that." Again the tearing laugh, the baby's body trembling slightly. "Jeremy didn't tell you to steal me, did he? His ideas, sometimes—"

"No," Colville said. "That was me. I thought, after the girl—"

"It's all right," the baby said. "It only complicates things—it wasn't the simplest way to proceed. It's not. Of course, you and I had to be brought together, to talk, so someone could tell you what to do next, where to go. You might say you don't need instruction, but you know you do."

Colville was still waking up; he watched the baby speak before he caught himself. Her lips moved, her mouth jerked slowly as if she were chewing, sucked as if she were nursing, but the motion, the shapes didn't match up with the words he heard. It was as if the voice had been dubbed, somehow, over the sounds a baby might make.

"This morning," she said, "first thing you need to do is go buy the maps. From the store where you went before, where you found those snowshoes and that ridiculous camouflage suit. You still have those things, I see. You'll need them."

He looked away: at the open bathroom door, light spilling out; at the row of glass bottles and rubber nipples on the counter; at the painting of an elk, hanging over the television, bugling as it stood next to a mountain stream.

"The maps," she was saying. "That special kind of map, on the grid. What's the word? The kind you had before."

"Topographic," he said.

"Yes," she said. "British Columbia, a place called Monashee Park, especially the area near Bill Fraser Lake. Way out in the wilderness, deep snow, you'll see. We've set up a cabin near there, and there's money and weapons buried. I'll show you on the map. You're resourceful, I know, Colville. I've seen it."

A voice shouted outside. A horn honked. Somewhere a door slammed.

"Isn't there enough money at the Heart?" he said. "The shelter there?"

"Perhaps that will be for later," she said. "Twenty, thirty years from now, when I'm ready. It will take some patience."

"I can be patient," he said.

"The store's not open yet," she said. "In the meantime, I'll tell you more, as long as I can stay awake. Your instructions, the future, how everything should unfold." Her voice drifted off, and she cried out for a moment before settling, continuing. "Monashee," she said. "There're no roads at Monashee. You have to walk in. There are bears, of course, though what is truly remarkable are the wolverines. We had some times with the wolverines."

"Thirty years?" he said.

"Maybe not so long," she said. "Maybe not. Prophecy is mercy and opportunity, after all. It's not set in stone."

With that, she pulled one of her hands loose from the blankets and began to open and close her fingers, right in front of her face. He waited for her to say more, but she was finished, had returned to being a baby. She stared at her fingers, transfixed by the wonder of their opening and closing.

25

COLVILLE COULD FEEL the warm weight of the baby, now, between his shoulder blades, her calm vibration easing through him. She slept as he walked along North 9th Street, closer to the elementary school. The sidewalk had been shoveled in front of some houses but remained icy and slick in front of others. He took each step with care. As powerful as she was, she was still fragile, the skin of her ears so thin that light shone through, her eyelashes long and delicate, her wrists thin and awkward. The blue veins forked so clearly beneath the white skin of her chest, and her forehead, her skull, the soft spot pulsing there.

Earlier this morning, when he had returned from the store, the baby was crying, hungry. She slept after drinking a bottle of formula; as she did, he whispered his way through a round of decrees, then organized the maps and snowshoes, the materials that he'd purchased. It was almost noon when she awakened. He spoke to her then, explaining his purchases, but she only cried. Her diaper was dirty; she was hungry. She didn't tell him, she just cried without tears, her face going red — this was how quickly and completely she shifted back and forth from being only a baby to being something, someone else. He'd fed her, he'd changed her diaper, and only then, just as it seemed she was falling asleep, did she begin to speak.

"Colville," she'd said. "Turn on the television. Turn down the sound. Good. Now listen. And if you look at me again while I'm talking, you won't hear another word."

There were a lot of instructions — some easy, some complicated enough that he had to write them down in his notebook; his eyes still fixed on the television, his words slanted away at all angles, overlapping each other. The coordinates on the map and the rest of the information, all the instructions he'd need to get from here to there. On the television screen, vans — news crews — were lined all up and down a snowy street. Newscasters talked into microphones, standing in front of Francine's house. There was no sign of Francine, no sign of Wells. At the bottom of the screen, words said ANOTHER ABDUCTION ON "UNLUCKY STREET": POLICE SAY TOO SOON TO ESTABLISH LINK. Next, a photograph of the baby who was at that moment in the room with him, talking, telling him that later this afternoon, when they went out, he could not wear his orange frame pack, that it might draw attention, might even be something people were looking for.

That was why he'd made the pack, the carrier that held her now, still sleeping on his back as he stepped aside to let the mailman pass on the narrow sidewalk. The pack was from a diagram, some pictures in the Boy Scout *Fieldbook,* something he'd always wanted to try. He'd taken an extra pair of his long pants, tied a cord tight around the cuff of each leg, and then folded the legs up, bent at the knee, and tied the cuffs through the belt loops beside the zipper. That way, the legs became shoulder straps. He cushioned the seat of the pants with a fleece vest and the down liner of his parka, so the baby would be warm and comfortable. Another cord fit through all the belt loops; pulled tight, it cinched the top of his pack closed, over the baby's sleeping face.

Now he leapt an icy puddle, slipped between parked cars, moving toward a square building of pale reddish brick. Longfellow Elementary School, its two entryways held up by concrete pillars, took up most of the block. He walked past without slowing; people sat in parked cars, parents waiting to pick up their children. The school day was almost over.

The baby sighed, shifted her weight, did not awaken. Along a chain-link fence, near some picnic tables, Colville slowed and turned, glancing back at the school's arched windows, up high, and all the rows below. Through one of those windows the sister was sitting, waiting, perhaps watching a clock. He hoped that her parents, her mother or father, weren't sitting nearby in one of these cars; he couldn't blame them if they were, given everything that had happened.

The bell rang, shaking the air, startling him. Almost immediately, children spilled from the doors of the school with their jackets half on or dragged along the ground, their high-pitched voices shouting. Horns honked. Car doors opened and closed.

He was afraid he might miss her, but he didn't want to move any closer to the children, to endanger himself. Voices shouted. He stood still. No one was looking at him. Cars swung slowly into the street, cutting through the slush, driving away. And there she was. Wearing a powder-blue coat and black snowmobile boots, a yellow knit cap over her messy dark hair.

"Della," he said.

Her eyes glanced up at his face, then quickly down again.

"Stranger," she said.

When she tried to walk past, around him, he stepped in front of her.

"I'll shout," she said. "I'll run away screaming."

"But I'm not a stranger," he said. "I know your name. You know me. I'm Colville. We talked to each other, up in the hills behind your house, about your sister."

"That doesn't mean you're not a stranger."

"I noticed your trampoline is gone," he said.

"Maybe," she said. "They might put it back up sometime."

Out in the playground, red plastic slides shaped like tubes, like hamster toys, stood out sharply against the snow, the empty basketball courts icy under bare trees.

"We used to play a game," she said. "Where I jumped and she was under the tramp so I could see her like a shadow and she tried to slap my feet when I jumped, where I landed."

"Let's keep walking," he said.

"That game made us really laugh," she said.

"Della," he said, "I need to talk with you, just a little bit, for just a little while."

"My mom's picking me up."

Fields stretched, tracked with footprints. Children walked across them in twos and threes. Brothers, sisters. Neighbors. A girl shouted Della's name and waved. Della waved back. Colville waited. The girl finally turned and kept walking away across the field.

"We can come right back here if you like," he said, slow to say anything now that Della had begun to walk alongside him.

"You stole my neighbor's dog," she said. "I saw you."

"I brought it back," he said. "I returned it to them just the other day."

"Are you wearing pants on your shoulders?"

"It's a backpack," he said. "I made it myself, yes, from a pair of pants."

Della looked at it suspiciously, but didn't ask any more questions. She scratched her nose with a bare hand, her right one; she wore a white-and-red knit glove on her left hand.

"I've been thinking of your sister," he said.

"This coat's hers, the one I wear." Della held one arm straight, pointed to her sleeve. "Sometimes people think I'm her."

Above, the sky was gray, a constant pressure pushing down. They crossed an intersection onto a quieter street. No cars slowed. No one came running out of the houses they passed. No voices shouted. Colville glanced all around; he felt Della's mother circling and circling, searching the area, winding closer.

"I've seen your sister," he said.

"Where?"

"She's far away. She's happy, very happy."

"Did you talk to her?"

"She's not coming back," he said. "I have to tell you that."

"She's not dead."

"No, she's not dead," Colville said. "You could think of her like she turned into another person, kind of."

Reaching into his pocket, he took out the leaf. It had dried a little, gone brittle with new lines, but the words *Hello Friend* still showed darkest, words scratched in. Colville held the leaf out and Della took it. She held it close to her face, squinting, then put it away in her pocket without saying anything.

"That's from where she is," he said. "The forest where she's living."

"Okay," Della said.

They continued to walk. She slid her boots in the slush, a raspy sound when the soles hit concrete. She pushed her black bangs up under her yellow wool hat.

"Did you hear about the baby?" he said.

"What?"

"Your neighbor's baby."

"Of course I did," she said. "Everyone knows."

"Knows what?"

"That someone took that baby."

"I see," he said, slowing, one hand on her shoulder before she shrugged it off. "Della," he said. "Did you tell anyone about the dog?"

"No," she said. "No one asked me."

A mail truck circled past; was this the second time? Chains rattled and rang from its tires.

"Where are you going to take me?" Della said.

"What?"

"To the forest?"

"No."

"Take me to where my sister is. You said she's happy, right? I want to go."

"I have the baby," he said.

"The baby?"

"Your neighbor's baby."

"You took it?"

"I need your help with her."

They went through the gate into the cemetery; here pine trees provided better cover. Colville stopped walking and Della did not run away. She turned to face him, to listen.

"It's that I'm not equipped," he said, "not really the person to take care of her. Not right now I'm not, anyway." He stammered, trying to get the words straight. "What it is is that the baby needs her parents and they need her. So what I need is, I need you to do is take her back to them."

Carefully, he bent one arm behind him and threaded it forward through the makeshift pack's strap, then swung it around. Loosening the cord through the belt loops, he lifted the baby out. She opened her milky eyes and gazed at him without a sound.

"That's her," Della said. "You had her in there this whole time?"

"Yes."

"I've never held a baby," she said, stepping back.

"Here. Careful. Support her head, but don't touch the top of it. It's easy."

A cold gust blew snow between the gravestones, around their feet. Colville could hear traffic, could see the colors of cars in his peripheral vision, in the spaces between the trees.

"So I'm supposed to say that I just found her?"

"You can say that if you want," Colville said. "See, she likes you."

"You don't want me to tell that it was you." Della squinted her bluish eyes, pursed her pale lips, then looked down again at the baby and smiled. "I'm going to say I found her right here," she said.

"Okay," he said.

"That's kind of true."

"It is."

"So now I just take her?"

"Yes."

Della turned and walked away, slowly between the grave-stones, careful of her footing, out the cemetery's far gate. Colville watched her go. Would they meet again? It seemed unlikely, yet they had already been brought together, and she was so young.

Careful not to walk across the graves, he retraced his steps: back onto the sidewalk, toward the motel, where he would gather his things and head north, into everything that would happen. Decrees looped around in his mind, the Violet Flame vibrating higher and faster. He had done so much; he had so much to do. And now, all around him, people. A man tossing handfuls of salt onto his driveway. Two women together, talking at the same time. The mailman again, and more children, walking home from school. As Colville passed, all of them looked in his direction. No one seemed to see him.

He turned back once, to watch Della, to see if she was still in sight. There she was, a block away, disappearing around a corner. Her pale blue coat, her yellow hat floated along, so bright against the snow.

Acknowledgments

Many members and former members of the Church Universal and Triumphant have generously shared their lives with me. The interviews and travels undertaken for this book made it a more interpersonal, bewildering, educational, and emotional experience than anything I have ever written. Some of the people who helped me most would rather not be acknowledged by name, as it might suggest a closer correspondence between their lives and these fictional pages than in fact exists. I understand and respect that, and still I want them to feel my true gratitude and respect for their energy and Light, good humor and patience with me.

Thanks to Genevieve, Henry, and Christian Lee; to Ian Scott, who shared his electricity; to Cheri Walsh; to Dr. Cathleen Mann, for trust and texts; to the late Kathleen Stanley.

My book is indebted to the writings of Elizabeth Clare Prophet, Mark Prophet, and many other texts of the church. I also relied on the "Green Books" of the "I AM Activity," by Godre Ray King (Guy Ballard) and the survival guides of Tom Brown, Jr. Other important texts included *The Art of War* by Sun-Tzu and the Boy Scouts' *Fieldbook*.

I am so fortunate to have lived above Paradise Valley during the shelter cycle, and luckier still to have worked for Virginia and Andy Anderson (who taught me the phrase "morphadite son of a bitch," and so much more). Spending time with Ginny and being back on the ranch these last few years was reason enough to write this book. Thank you. And to the amazing Julie and Hannibal Anderson and their family, always.

Thanks to Chico Hot Springs, the best base camp a person could ever wish for. And to the Reed College Dean's Office and English Department, for key funding. All gratitude to Jason Parker for generous and dexterous website assistance. A debt to Trina Marmarelli, for last-minute cartography.

Jim Rutman, it is difficult to really know what is your deal and how you got this way, but I can only try to express how wisely you punished me, and to wonder at how vast your belief and patience are. I won't forget. Thanks also to Adelaide Livingston Wainwright at Sterling Lord, student and teacher.

Adrienne Brodeur, my editor, has encouraged me in friendship and in fiction for fifteen years. Visibly, invisibly. I am all gratitude and so fortunate.

Much appreciation for the patience, enthusiasm, and intelligence of all at Houghton Mifflin Harcourt for helping bring this book into the world.

Cara Warner and Ariana Boffey tirelessly and enthusiastically transcribed thirty-plus hours of interviews for me. Necessary.

At different times, these smart and kind people read (often extremely long) drafts of this novel and told me what they thought: Kate Bredeson, Ben Lazier, Rachel Mercer, Tamara Metz, Amy Smith, Maya West. Thanks, friends. May you pass every test, as Saint Germain would say.

Here at home, my girls — everything. So grateful to Ida Akiko and Miki Frances, for slowing me down (and sometimes breaking me down), for showing me with their hearts what I was trying to do with my head.

And I would not be me if Ella Vining were not Ella Vining, every single day.